Francis Beaumont
and Julie Bozza

A Night with the Knight of the Burning Pestle

Full of Mirth and Delight

LIBRAtiger

Published by LIBRAtiger

ISBN: 978-0-9955465-2-3

Text: © Julie Bozza 2017
Proofreading and line-editing: Two Marshmallows
    twomarshmallows.net
Editor: Fiona Pickles, Manifold Press
    manifoldpress.co.uk
Book format: © Julie Bozza 2017
Set in Adobe Caslon

Cover image and design: © Jeffrey Nguyen 2017
    jeffreynguyen.net

libra-tiger.com | juliebozza.com

Contents

Introduction

My editor's first response after reading this story was to describe it as "a love-letter to the play and to the whole theatrical experience". I'm delighted that my love shone through so clearly!

My presentation of the intertwining plots of Francis Beaumont's play *The Knight of the Burning Pestle*, however, may not be quite so clear without a brief introduction. I promise there are no spoilers here, but if you would prefer to jump right in, please feel free to go right ahead.

Meanwhile, for the rest of us! In Beaumont's play, two Citizens – the grocer George and his wife Nell – along with their apprentice Rafe, have come to the theatre to see a play called *The London Merchant*. The three of them sit down in the audience, as if they were regular punters. A few lines into *The London Merchant*'s Prologue, however, George leaps to his feet and protests. He's tired of these new-fangled city comedies which joke at the expense of good, honest merchants. Instead, George wants an old-fashioned tale of chivalry and adventure.

When the boy speaking the Prologue protests that they can't very well interrupt their play, and in any case there's no one available to present such scenes, Nell suggests that Rafe take on the part. This is grudgingly agreed to, for the sake of peace. Rafe is dubbed the Knight of the Burning Pestle, and his 'impromptu' scenes are performed between the rehearsed scenes. Thus we have two plays unfolding within a play, with commentary and constant interruptions from the Citizens, who remain in the audience throughout.

If that all sounds a little confusing, well … it is! And the confusion actually becomes one of the delights of the play, both on the page and on the stage.

The London Merchant's story features Jasper, apprentice to the merchant Venturewell. Jasper is in love with his master's daughter, Luce, and she loves him, too – but Venturewell has another, far richer suitor in mind for her: the foppish Humphrey.

Meanwhile, Jasper's family are in turmoil. His father, Old Master Merrythought, is a carefree soul who does nothing but sing all day. They are down to their last few shillings, and Mistress Merrythought is at her wits' end. Jasper will want his inheritance so he can marry Luce, but his mother is determined that the little she has managed to scrape together will all go to her younger, favoured son, Michael.

Meanwhile, in *The Knight of the Burning Pestle*, Rafe recruits a squire and a page, and heads off to adventures in Waltham Forest (to the north-east of London city). Here he encounters not only a dangerous giant, but also Mistress Merrythought, Michael and other characters from *The London Merchant* – and so the two plays interweave delightfully.

Adding a great deal of hilarity to the mix, the characters in *The London Merchant* sometimes react to the ongoing confusion in character and sometimes as the actors, who are (naturally enough!) frustrated and annoyed at their play being usurped.

In telling this story, I wrapped yet another layer around

the whole, featuring Dale and Topher, the two actors who play Rafe and Jasper, and following them and the rest of the cast backstage.

Phew!

I should add for the scholars among you that I have taken a few liberties with Beaumont's text, paring back some of the scenes and speeches, and sometimes updating the language. My goal was to convey the essentials to a modern audience as smoothly as possible, while trying to maintain the immersive experience of watching the play itself.

The largest liberty I took was turning the Citizen George into Georgiana. Also, I felt it was unnecessarily confusing that Rafe's page was also named George, so I renamed him Frank.

To conclude at last: I had a great deal of fun writing this story, and can only hope you'll have just as much fun reading it.

◆

Acknowledgements

With ardent thanks to the Sam Wanamaker Playhouse, artistic director Dominic Dromgoole, and director Adele Thomas, for introducing me to *The Knight of the Burning Pestle*, via two wonderfully riotous productions in 2014. Thank you also to Camilla Imperiali and Catherine Walker of the Friends office, for helping appease my curiosity about the SWP, and to Philip Milnes-Smith of the Globe Library and Archive for letting me re-live the KBP experience. Any mistakes or infelicities in how I've staged this play in their beautiful Playhouse are, of course, entirely my own.

I consulted a few different texts, but am particularly grateful to the very thorough *Revels Plays* edition, edited by Sheldon P. Zitner (2004).

With thanks also to the wonderful vibrant overwhelming city of London. Love is the only way to know you.

But most of all, thank you to Francis Beaumont, who wrote this play in 1607 at the age of 23. I am in awe of this glorious early-modern post-modern mash-up, and I've loved working with it. Even though I remain a tad amazed at my own presumption.

◆

The Knight of
the Burning Pestle

The Speakers' Names

Georgiana, citizen of London and grocer

Nell, wife to Georgiana

Rafe, apprentice grocer and sometime Knight of the Burning Pestle; played by **Dale**

The London Merchant

Sam, who speaks the prologue, dances and sings

Venturewell, merchant

Jasper, apprentice to Venturewell; played by **Topher**

Luce, daughter to Venturewell; played by **Verity**

Humphrey, friend to Venturewell and suitor for Luce; played by **Jeremy**, a Celebrity

Mistress Merrythought, mother to Jasper

Michael, younger brother of Jasper

Old Master Merrythought, father to Jasper

The Knight of the Burning Pestle

Tim, a squire

Frank, a dwarf

Sundry others, including: a tapster; a host; a barber; a messenger; various serving boys; four men to carry a coffin

And featuring: **Pompiona**, daughter to the King of Moldavia

◆

Backstage

"Did we ever work out what this play is about?" asked Topher.

"You're asking me *now*?" Dale retorted with a mild sense of outrage that was mostly feigned. "It's our last show!"

"Better late than never."

"We're going on in a minute."

"In thirty minutes," Topher quietly replied.

"*Seriously.*"

They were sitting in their corner of the men's dressing room, each at his own table – at right angles and far too often at cross purposes. Dale leant in to shoot Topher a fiery look via the reflections in their mirrors. Not that Dale would let Topher rattle him, of course. The friendly repartee they shared was generally for real, and the less good-natured niggling was usually for display purposes only. Dale knew that Topher knew that for Dale the work came first, and if Topher went too far, Dale would simply shut him out.

Topher finished off his make-up, and then tended to his hair with his usual slapdash though effective method: he ran his hands back over his hair to smooth it down, before pushing his fingers up through his fringe so it stood from his forehead with rakish charm. They couldn't use hairspray or certain kinds of gel due to the stage being lit by beeswax candles, but Topher had found some kind of uninflammable product that he swore he loved even more than his regular brand. Dale hadn't had the same luck in finding a replacement for his usual stuff – but then, he was playing the innocent dork as opposed to the romantic lead, so it didn't matter very much if his hair was rather a shambles.

That smug git Topher was now lounging back in his chair, swivelling it halfway towards Dale and meeting his gaze from over Dale's shoulder, via Dale's mirror. They were both mostly dressed already. Topher had only to slip on the boots and doublet of his Jacobean-era costume, and Dale was lacking only his modern-day jacket and shoes. They were in plenty of time. But now that Dale considered him properly, he found that Topher actually seemed quite pensive – which was a tad alarming when Topher's default setting was usually to look rather pleased with himself. Dale eyed Topher's reflection with a caution that no doubt Topher could read. But Dale said nothing.

Eventually, Topher remarked, with an edge to his overly casual tone, "Our last show, eh?"

Dale made a noncommittal sound that Topher could take as agreement if he wished.

"Are we going to celebrate in the same way as before?"

Dale froze. "I thought we'd agreed –" he found himself whispering fiercely, before grinding to a halt. He didn't need to state the obvious. *I thought we'd agreed on professional.* He was *this* close to grabbing up the nearest thing to hand, spinning in his chair, and throwing it at the insufferably beautiful bastard. The beautifully insufferable bastard. The nearest thing would have been his half-full mug of tea, Dale noted, which would have made a decent dent in Topher's skull, and stained his character's white shirt as well.

After a long, still moment, Dale forced himself to shift in his chair. He checked his foundation in the mirrors, and then leaned close to apply eyeliner along each lower lid. Once he was done, Dale took the opportunity to glance casually across the rest of the dressing room, and was relieved to see the other guys at a distance, all minding their own business. Then Dale sat back and considered the overall effect of his hair and makeup with a pretence of satisfaction.

Topher wasn't satisfied. That much was clear from his sour expression and slumped shoulders. "No," he muttered, turning away. "Didn't think so."

It had been months since they'd last worked together – almost a year, now Dale thought about it. Almost a year since they'd parted, with a handshake and (surely!) an unspoken agreement that gentlemen neither tell nor ask for second helpings. Dale had thought the past was safely in the past, despite the occasional crackle of tension between them when they'd met up again during the read-through and rehearsals. But perhaps he'd been wrong about that.

At least they were both too professional to let it affect the show. Topher stood now, and stepped around to face Dale in order to hold out his hand to shake. "Sorry. Pretend I was too couth to say anything."

"Of course." Dale shook the proffered hand – and very deliberately fought down the sense-memory of that hand curved tenderly around his flank then slipping down to shape itself hard around his hip.

"See you out there, then."

Dale nodded, and offered a half-smile – though

Topher was already out the door, with his doublet and boots hastily grasped, and the effort was wasted on him. Dale let out a sigh instead.

Well. He'd thought Topher had become quite oblivious to Dale's sparse charms. He'd assumed their long-ago encounter had meant as little to Topher as it was supposed to. The whole stupid thing had been insignificant, of course. A slow growth and then a quick release of unwanted tension, that was all it had been, there was no point in romanticising it, and in any case there was no room in Dale's life for anything more. If Topher had once had thoughts of changing that, surely it was clear by now that Dale was perfectly happy was he was. It had been nothing, really.

For a while there, though … Only for a short while, of course, and probably only because Topher had woken him up with coffee in the morning, exactly the way Dale liked it best … For a little while, Dale had to admit to himself that he'd been fooled into thinking it meant the whole world.

◆

"This is your quarter call," the Stage Manager announced over the sound system. "Once more with feeling for our final night, people. We're opening the house. Citizens and Rafe to the foyer, please."

Dale headed out through the green room – no sign of Topher – then down to reception and the stage door, and outside into the service yard. He slipped through the security gate as invisibly as possible, then around the corner into New Globe Walk, where he segued into the slightly anxious, slightly thrilled air of his character, and filed into the theatre's foyer along with the punters. A moment later he was joined by the production's Citizens, Georgiana and Nell, who'd been picking up their tickets at the collection desk. The three of them shared a grin that worked on at least two levels – as actors tired and giddy at the end of a three-week run, and as characters excited by a night out at the theatre.

One of the serving staff from the café bar came over with a tray of beers in plastic tumblers, and they took them gratefully. It was only the no-alcohol stuff, of course, but they had to pretend it was deliciously refreshing.

Georgiana and Nell talked together about the inconsequentialities of their business week, while Dale – who was playing Rafe, their apprentice – remained self-effacingly quiet. He was wearing Rafe's 'earnest though slightly dim' face, even though he was fairly sure that only a few of the punters had twigged to their presence. He sipped at his beer.

The three of them were dressed in regular modern clothes. Georgiana, the well-to-do late-thirties grocer was cool, slim and striking in her dark blue business suit, ivory shirt, and expensively understated silver necklace. Her beloved wife Nell was young and blonde, warm and buxom in a tightly-fitted green dress with sequins, and adorned with excessive amounts of gold jewellery that made her shine.

In contrast, Rafe was in blue stovepipe jeans, a sage green t-shirt, blue-and-brown trainers, and an old much-loved brown leather jacket. When it came to costumes,

Dale was the most comfortable he'd ever been. As for Rafe, he wanted to be smart-casual, but was basically too clueless, too poor, and too earnest a young man to ever quite pull an outfit together into a look.

Most of the punters had filtered through into the Sam Wanamaker Playhouse by now, so Georgiana, Nell and Rafe joined the tail of the queue and shuffled along. Georgiana handed over their tickets, just like anyone else, and they were directed towards their seats in the front row of the Pit.

"On my god!" Nell cried loudly as they entered the Playhouse proper, and took a look around. Jacobean music filled the air, as sweet to the ears as the place itself was fragrant to the eyes. "It's like a pretty little box of bling!"

There were snatches of laughter from the punters at her reaction – whether they thought her a regular member of the audience, or knew better, it was all much the same at this point. Georgiana strolled onwards with her long-legged stride, confident and pleased. Rafe followed afterwards, looking somewhat awed, and instinctively stepping in time to the spritely tune.

The Sam Wanamaker Playhouse had been described as a 'jewel box of a theatre' right from the start. The seating and pillars were raw oak, but the ceiling was painted to show the Heavens, and the façade of the tiring house at the back of the stage was particularly beautiful – elegantly sumptuous – painted in olive green with gilded details. To add to the magic, the stage was lit only by beeswax candles, which bathed everything in a warm glow and gave a pearly sheen to every reflecting surface.

At the back of the stage, hanging to the left of the

central double doors to the tiring house, was a board on which 'The London Merchant' was written in a clear, flowing script. That was the play they were here to watch.

In a gallery above the façade and the doors, musicians in Jacobean dress played period instruments, entertaining the audience as it gathered, talked and finally settled, as had been the practice when these plays were originally presented. Apparently, at some productions in the early 1600s, such concerts had lasted an hour.

Georgiana, Nell and Rafe took their seats in the front row, with the latter two still gawping at the magnificent theatre. Dale carefully maintained Rafe's dimness – which wasn't all that challenging, for Topher kept returning to his mind, unbidden, and when Dale thought about Topher, he felt even dimmer than Rafe.

After a long moment, Nell lifted her phone, and took a photo of the stage. She was immediately told off by an usher (with a polite but firm "There's no photography allowed, madam"), so Nell slipped her phone away into her handbag, but didn't bother looking at all repentant.

As soon as the usher's back was turned, out came the phone again, and the photo was shared via the @CitizenNell Twitter account. There were obviously a few punters in the know, because a moment later notifications chimed from their phones – accompanied by a little nervous laughter, and some tsk-ing from audience members who weren't in on the joke. Someone was cheeky enough to reply to Nell's Tweet; she read it and laughed appreciatively, looking around to see if she could spot them.

The usher approached again, and Georgiana added a look of mild reproof, so Nell switched the phone to silent and tucked it away. "Okay, yeah, we'd better behave," Nell said, sharing a half-real, half-mock grimace of exasperation with the surrounding audience.

"Thank you, madam," the usher said courteously, before withdrawing to her allotted station.

"*The London Merchant*," Nell read out in a loud voice. "That's you, innit, Georgie? You're a London merchant."

"Hush, cony," Georgiana responded, a little irritably. Not that she seemed annoyed with her wife as such, but she folded her arms tightly across her chest, and stared hard at the back of the stage.

The very last audience members to arrive were a tall, skinny guy and a little man. There was some argument about their ticket – for they had only one between them – but soon the skinny guy's rear was perched on the very end of a bench seat in the front row of a Lords' Room to one side of the stage, and the little fellow was sitting on his knees. It was perfectly apparent that the little man wouldn't have been able to see properly if sitting on his own – and the skinny guy seemed utterly uninterested in the whole thing, as if resigned to his role as supplementary furniture – so no one seemed to grudge them despite all the fuss. Except maybe for Georgiana, who couldn't suppress a *tsk*.

At last the modern-day house lights faded, and the tune finished with a flourish. Georgiana sat up even straighter, her shoulders sharp and stiff, while Nell leaned forward in growing excitement. *The London Merchant* was about to begin.

◆

Induction

The main, double doors of the tiring house were opened, and Sam entered, dressed in a smart though understated Jacobean costume complete with ruff, doublet, breeches and hose. He moved with a dancer's poise, stepping to the front centre of the stage, where he took a dramatic stance, and began speaking the Prologue.

> "From all that's near the court, from all that's great,
> Within the compass of the city-walls,
> We now have brought our scene –"

Georgiana had gone from mildly irritated to utterly exasperated in less than three lines, and now she could no longer contain herself. She sprang to her feet, and with one stride was at the foot of the stage with her hands on her hips, glaring up at Sam. "Now, hold it right there!"

"What?!" squawked Sam. A few members of the audience gasped, but otherwise most of them seemed to have caught their breath in shock. Those who were already in the know were deadly curious to see how this played out.

Sam tried to restart – "We now have brought –" but Georgiana cut him off.

"Seven years ago I swore I would never set foot in a theatre again, for in each and every play you mock the citizens of this fine city." Georgiana gestured angrily at the board hanging on the tiring house façade. "And I see that nothing has changed, for now you call your play *The London Merchant*. Down with your title, young sir! Down with your title!"

There was a long moment's silence. The musicians watched curiously from their gallery, and one of the serving boys poked his head out through the curtains behind the main doors of the tiring house – before being hauled back out of sight with a little cry of protest.

Eventually, Sam asked, "Are you a citizen of this noble city?"

"I am."

"And a guild member, too, I warrant?"

Georgiana, always of tall bearing, drew herself up even further. "I am a member, boy, of the Worshipful Company of Grocers."

"It's a liverary company," Nell remarked to Rafe and to the people in the row immediately behind them.

(From the corner of his eye, Dale saw one of the audience members mouth a sceptical 'Liverary … ?' to her neighbour, and roll her eyes. But judging from the amused smiles, everyone else seemed to get the joke.)

"It's not a guild," Nell was blithely continuing. "She hates it when you get that wrong!"

Sam inclined his head in a display of politeness. "So, madam grocer –"

"She's got a whole string of grocery shops, does my Georgie!" Nell proudly added.

Georgiana shot Nell a fondly quelling look, while Sam tried again. "So, good madam grocer, I swear by your sweet face and favour, we intend no abuse to the city."

"Oh, don't you? I say that you do. If you didn't want to

play the knave, then you could have chosen to play *The Legend of Dick Whittington and his Cat*, or *The Life and Death of Sir Thomas Gresham, with the Building of the Royal Exchange*, or *The Story of Queen Eleanor, with the Rearing of London Bridge upon Woolsacks*."

Sam had no immediate answer for this, but after a moment managed, "You seem to be an *understanding* woman –" with a broad sweep of his arm to indicate the pun. "What would you have us do, madam?"

Georgiana slapped her palm against the wooden stage with a hollow thud. "Why, present something that honours the people of the city."

Sam let out a guffaw. "What do you say to *The Life and Death of Fat Drake, with the Repairing of Fleet-Privies?*" Which was a nonsense, of course.

Jasper quietly appeared from behind the curtains, and stood there watching, outside the light cast directly by the candles, with his arms crossed and his stance impatient. The serving boy along with the messenger boy sneaked out to peer around him at these goings-on.

Drawing herself up even taller, Georgiana stiffly responded to Sam, "I do *not* like it. But I *will* have a citizen, and he – or she – shall be of my own trade."

"Oh, you should have asked it a month ago," Sam cried in exasperation. "Our play is ready to begin now."

Dale had noticed that the audience, interestingly enough, always seemed a little restless around this point – as if they were impatient to see the actual play – or, indeed, any play. As if they were reflecting that such interruptions would have been utterly detestable in real life. Dale wondered if Francis Beaumont's first audience had been alienated by the conceit, no matter how ingenious, and that had led to the play's failure. It had only been produced for one performance in Beaumont's lifetime – in the Blackfriars theatre on which the Sam Wanamaker Playhouse was based.

Georgiana, of course, continued undeterred by Sam's refusal. "I *will* have a grocer, and he – or she – shall do admirable things."

"Like what?!"

"I will have him – or –"

Nell was on the edge of her seat with excitement, holding up her hand, bursting for attention. "Georgie! Georgie!"

"Peace, Nell," Rafe murmured.

"Hold *your* peace, Rafe," she retorted. "I know what I'm doing. – Georgie! Georgie!"

Georgiana had turned towards her. "What is it, cony?"

"Let him kill a lion with a pestle, Georgie. Let him kill a lion with a pestle!"

"And so he shall," Georgiana replied, before turning back to address Sam. "I'll have him kill a lion with a pestle."

From behind Sam, Jasper threw his hands up in a 'What the … ?' gesture. How on earth were they meant to stage such a thing?

Nell was too restless with excitement to be seated any longer; she got up and joined Georgiana at the feet of the flummoxed Sam. "You'll all excuse me, I'm sure," Nell said, addressing the audience and meeting the gaze of anyone who'd let her. "I know I'm a troublesome thing, but I'm a stranger here. I was never at one of these plays before. I should have seen *Jane Shore* once – and my Georgie promised me, any time this past year, to take me to *The Bold Beauchamps*, but it never quite happened. So, be patient with me."

Georgiana took Nell's hand and lifted it, as if about to formally escort her back to their seats. But first she said to Sam, "Begin as soon as you will, boy, and let the grocer do rare things."

Sam was about ready to tear his hair out. "But, madam, we don't have anyone to play him. Everyone has a part already, and some are doubling roles as it is."

Nell, of course, had the answer to that. "Georgie, Georgie! Oh. My. God. Let Rafe play him! Rafe will be as brilliant as any of them, and you know it!"

"An excellent idea, wife. – Go up on the stage, Rafe."

Rafe startled, but didn't even get to his feet.

Jasper – the leading man of *The London Merchant* – put his hands on his hips, and grimaced in irritation at the notion of sharing the candlelight.

"I'll tell you all," Georgiana declared to the audience, "let them lend our Rafe a costume and props, and you'll get your ticket's worth of entertainment, I swear it."

"Go on, Rafe," Nell urged. As Rafe finally stood, and walked up the steps to the stage as reverently as if he were about to take communion, Nell continued, "Oh, *do* lend him a costume, boy. My missus is right," she declared to the audience. "Rafe often does a scene at our house after dinner, even though all our guests cry out that they are not worthy to hear him. Or he'll tell a rousing speech, and leave us quaking. And if my child is being naughty, I'll cry 'Rafe comes, Rafe comes!' to her, and she'll be quiet as a lamb." Nell gestured towards Rafe. "Stand tall, Rafe, and stir them with a speech."

Dale struck a heroic pose, gazing off into the distance beyond the Playhouse walls – and Rafe provided a slightly inaccurate snippet of Hotspur from Shakespeare's *Henry IV, Part 1*. Dale delivered the lines with a simple clarity that reflected Rafe's pure-hearted innocence.

> "By Heaven, methinks, it were an easy leap
> To pluck bright honour from the pale-faced moon;
> Or dive into the bottom of the sea,
> Where never fathom-line touched any ground,
> And pluck up drowned honour from the lake of
>   Hell."

"Didn't I tell you, boy?" Georgiana demanded.

Indeed, Rafe had made such an impression that their Mistress Merrythought from *The London Merchant* was peering around the left-hand door at the back of the stage – and she obviously liked what she saw. Meanwhile, the little man in the audience, still perched on the skinny guy's knees, was leaning forward with his hands on the oak balustrade, staring agog. Only Jasper was unimpressed, throwing up his hands in frustration at his play being so derailed.

"Rafe has played before," Nell proudly added. "Not that I saw it, but Georgie had him play Mucedorus at the guildhall for the wardens of our liverary company." (This time her tongue tripped a little over the extra syllable, but Nell wasn't the sort to doubt herself.)

"All right, all right!" Sam cried in surrender. He

gestured towards the main doors that led to the tiring house behind the stage – doing a double-take with a shudder when he saw Jasper standing there glaring at them, though Sam did not change his mind. He turned back to the Citizens. "Your man shall have a costume, if he will go in."

Jasper withdrew in despair, impatiently ushering the two boys backstage ahead of him.

"Go in, Rafe," said Georgiana. "And if you love me, do us grocers proud."

Rafe ducked his head in a bow to his two mistresses, and strode off through the central doors, slipping past the heavy dark curtains that hid the ramshackle reality of the tiring house from the audience.

◆

Backstage

As Dale's eyes adjusted to the relative dimness, Mistress Merrythought stepped quietly past him heading back to the green room. They exchanged a brief smile, and then she was gone. But Dale paused, sensing that something was awry.

Behind him on the stage, muffled by the curtains, Sam was asking the Citizens what they would have Rafe's play called.

"*The Grocer's Honour*," was Georgiana's reply.

With a leer in his voice, Sam suggested, "What about *The Knight of the Burning Pestle?*"

"Brilliant!" cried Nell, completely missing the less savoury innuendo.

"Let it be so," Georgiana declared.

With a start, Dale realised that Topher was pressed back into a shadowed corner of the backstage area, almost as if trying to avoid Dale. Topher had always waited in the tiring house at this point, ready for the first scene in Act One which featured Jasper and Venturewell – but he'd never tried to hide himself away before now.

When he realised he'd been seen, Topher took a step forward – and, for a moment as he emerged into the dim light, he appeared quite woebegone.

Dale instinctively stepped forward in sympathetic response.

From the audience, Nell was loudly demanding to know whether the musicians in the gallery above had accordions.

"Accordions!" cried Sam in shock. "No."

"Rafe plays a dramatic part," said Georgiana, "and he must needs have accordions. I'll pay for them myself, rather than be without."

"So you are like to be," said Sam.

"Why, and so I will be. There's two score for you," she said, taking out her wallet and handing up two twenty-pound notes.

Sam took the money, but apparently felt obliged to point out, "We'll never find any at this late hour."

"Aw …" Nell sulked. "But these guys," she continued, indicating the musicians, "can still play the 'Chicken Dance' for us, right?"

And after a moment's further encouragement, the musicians gamely struck up a shambolic version of the 'Chicken Dance' on their medieval instruments. There was much laughter and an accompaniment of clapping from the audience, and Nell of course was doing the moves, flapping her wings and shaking her beautifully ample booty, to everyone's delight.

Not that Dale was watching anything other than Topher's mutable face which had slowly formed a reluctant smile. "There's *one* thing I won't miss," Topher said in a low voice, gesturing up to indicate the music.

"The worst earworm in the world, that song," Dale quietly agreed.

Topher's eyes glinted in the light, perhaps from humour. Perhaps not. Dale was determined not to find out.

Sam was at last allowed to deliver the Prologue for *The*

London Merchant. The quiet closing of a door indicated that their Venturewell was making his way through from the green room, ready to take the stage with Jasper.

Dale's heart suddenly thudded large and urgent. "You all right?" he whispered, stepping closer to Topher.

"Of course!" Topher protested, his expression clearing so that he looked calmly and confidently happy.

Almost all the world assumed that this happy, handsome confidence was the real Topher. Dale knew better. But then, he also knew better than to distract Topher any further at this point.

Venturewell joined them with a nod of greeting to each, absently rubbing his hands together as if hardly aware of his own anxiety.

Dale leaned close to Topher's ear and hissed the Italian good luck charm they'd borrowed: "*In bocca al lupo!*" (In the mouth of the wolf!)

Topher grinned, and responded, "*Crepi il lupo.*" (May the wolf die.)

After another exchange with the Citizens, Sam burst through the central doors into the tiring house, almost running into Dale – while Venturewell and Jasper were already entering the stage through the smaller door on the left.

◆

Act One

"Sirrah," declared Venturewell to Jasper with haughty dignity, "I'll make you know you are my prentice. You were nothing when you came here, but I gave you food and shelter, and I trusted you with all my dealings both here and on the seas, in foreign markets. I made you anew." He concluded with some force: "But I never charged you to love your master's daughter! I have found a wealthy husband for her, and I take it, sir, that you have not. I will remind you again, that you are nothing more than a merchant's agent."

Jasper was all bright-eyed sincerity and loved-up energy. "Sir, I happily confess I am yours, bound by both love and duty to your service. I have worked hard for you, and it has all been to my own profit. Sir, I am a humble and temperate man. If your virtuous daughter loves me, it is her own choice – and you cannot think she would rather choose that unnatural fellow you mean to match her with."

Dale had not returned to the green room, but loitered backstage, peering out through the little grate in the right-hand door – invisible to the audience – that allowed him to watch what was happening on stage. Topher was proving yet again that he was born to play the romantic lead. It wasn't only his classically handsome looks, but his honest happy fervour, which was a delight to daughters and a danger to those fathers who had other plans. (Or to anyone else who had other plans, for that matter, Dale grumbled to himself.)

This father, in particular, remained unconvinced. "I know how all this shall be cured," said Venturewell. "I discharge you from my house and service. Take your liberty!" And Venturewell stalked off the stage.

Jasper remained, to reflect sadly, "These are the fair rewards for those who love! Oh, you who live in freedom, I trust you never experience the toil of a mind led by desire!"

Dale continued to gaze upon Topher, though he couldn't have explained why. Usually there was a giddy last-day-of-school feel about the final performance in the run of a play. Dale, however, felt quite sombre.

It was just as well that Verity, who was playing Jasper's love interest Luce, was her usual bright self. "How are you, my friend?" Luce asked as she made her entrance. "Struck by my father's thunder?"

"Struck dead, unless you have the remedy," Jasper replied. "I am no longer your father's."

"But mine."

"But yours, and only yours, I am. You dare be constant still?"

"Oh, fear me not!"

Jasper asked somewhat more urgently, "You know my rival?"

"Yes, and love him dearly – even as I love an ague or foul weather. I pray you, Jasper, fear him not."

"Then you remember the plot we both agreed on?"

"Yes," Luce reassured him, "and I'll perform my part exactly."

"I desire no more. Farewell, and keep my heart with yours."

"I'll ne'er forsake it." And Luce exited through the left-hand door, while Jasper left the stage through the main doors.

All this while, in the front row of the Pit, Nell had been restless and bored, fidgeting with her phone, tangling and untangling her distractingly glinting necklaces, rummaging through her handbag – while Georgiana grew more and more impatient, unable to suppress a hand tapping almost silently against one narrow thigh. Dale figured Francis Beaumont had deliberately written these scenes long, partly to give the audience time to get their minds around the whole two-plays-within-a-play thing, and partly to provide provocation to the Citizens.

"Fie upon those two young infidels!" Georgiana burst out now, getting to her feet. "What ingratitude is that to show to a good master, and a good father?"

"Rafe will come soon," Nell reassured her, "and he'll be far more interesting, and he'll do brave deeds." She also stood. "I know! Let's ask that young bloke when we can expect Rafe."

"Yes, do so," Georgiana agreed.

Nell rapped her knuckles on the stage, which made a distinctive hollow sound. "Oi! Pretty boy! Come out here."

After an expectant pause, Sam peered out through the main doors, and then ventured forth, his body language cramped as if trying not to draw attention to himself. "Yes, madam?"

"Is Rafe ready?" Nell demanded.

"He will be presently."

Ah. Dale had been so distracted, he'd almost forgotten about his next cue. He quickly shrugged off his jacket and heeled off his trainers, and then poked his head out of the right-hand door. "Pssst …" With an attempt at discretion, Rafe pointed at the little man and the skinny guy in the audience, and then beckoned for them to come to him.

"Rafe!" cried Nell.

"Rafe!" cried Georgiana. "Whatever are you doing?"

Rafe sidled out onto the stage, embarrassed to be caught. "Mistress, as you know full well, every knight must have a squire, and a dwarf as his page, to go on adventures with."

"It is true," Georgiana agreed. "And have they furnished you with companions as well as a costume and props?"

"No, mistress, every actor here already has their part, and so I thought these two may assist." He indicated the two audience members.

The little guy was delighted by the idea, and promptly somersaulted over the balustrade and onto the stage, where he landed on both feet with a flourish. A smattering of laughter and applause from the audience was met with a sweeping low bow and a bit of happy strutting, which of course only encouraged more appreciation.

"Nah," said the skinny guy. "You can 'ave him, but I'm not into it. Find someone else."

"Come on, Tim," the little man encouraged. He lifted a hand for Rafe to shake. "Hi, I'm Frank."

"Hello, Frank. I'm Rafe."

"Come *on*, Tim."

"I really don't fancy it," the skinny guy complained. But eventually, with much rolling of his eyes, Tim slowly clambered over onto the stage and let Rafe shake his hand in greeting. Then Rafe ushered his new companions backstage, one eager and one massively reluctant.

Sam had been watching all this with hands on hips. "Well?" he asked once the stage was clear again. "May we continue with our play now?"

"You may," Georgiana graciously replied, oblivious to his sarcasm.

◆

While Rafe and his two new companions were backstage getting ready for their first scene, *The London Merchant* continued with Venturewell talking to Humphrey, the friend he'd chosen as suitor for Luce.

"Come, sir, she's yours. Upon my faith, she's yours, you have my hand," vowed Venturewell. "My wanton prentice, that like a bladder blew himself full with love, I have let out, and sent him to discover new masters yet unknown."

Being the father's choice and not the daughter's, Humphrey was of course rather dull and safe in character, though bright in plumage. And he was pretentious, too, demonstrated by the fact he was the only character to always speak in rhyming couplets.

> "It shall be known, however you do deem,
> I am of gentle blood, and gentle seem."

He went on to declare his love for Luce, laboriously using a blood pudding as a simile – and all in neatly rhymed verse, of course. Not that Humphrey was entirely unattractive, as he was played by Jeremy, who was tall and charming, and who almost – *almost* – managed to carry off the clothes of a vain Jacobean dandy.

In the midst of Venturewell and Humphrey's exchange, Nell could be heard to cry from the Pit, "Georgiana! Georgiana!"

The action on stage ground to a halt.

"What is it, mouse?" her wife complacently replied.

"Georgie, isn't he that bloke? You know the one. That Bloke! I'm sure I've seen him on the telly."

"Hush now, lamb."

"Oh, he is a pretty fellow, though, ain't he? I'm sure he's Somebody, you know."

Humphrey – or rather the actor playing Humphrey – was visibly basking in the praise, and the audience were happily chuckling away. The joke was, of course, that Jeremy was the production's Celebrity Name, cast not only for his talent and looks but also his ability to boost ticket sales.

"Hey," cried Nell to Jeremy, jumping to her feet and waving to demand his attention. "I know! You were on *EastEnders* once or twice, weren't you?"

Aghast! Jeremy drew himself up in a huff. Not that the *real* Jeremy was a snob about soaps, ads, voice-work and such things – god only knew that working actors couldn't afford to be fussy – but he milked the joke for what it was worth, and the audience obviously thought it hilarious.

When they quietened down a bit, Georgiana patted the empty seat beside her. "Come now, cony, sit down. He is pretty enough as fellows go, I agree – but when Rafe comes, lamb …"

"Oh yes," Nell said with a happy sigh. "When Rafe comes!"

And so the play was permitted to continue. "Well, sir," Venturewell said to Humphrey, "you have my love and my consent; now you must seek my daughter's. Woo her boldly! – and then wed her when you please."

> "I take your gentle offer, and withal
> Yield love again for love reciprocal."

Venturewell called Luce out to the stage, and before retiring instructed her, "Welcome this gentleman to our home – and don't be contrary."

Luce bobbed a mock-obedient curtsey at her departing father, and then turned to Humphrey with an expectantly arched brow.

Humphrey struck a gallant pose.

> "Fair Mistress Luce, how do you? Are you well?
> Give me your hand, and then I pray you tell
> How doth your little sister and your brother;
> And whether you love me or any other."

Everyone winced at the poetry of which Humphrey was so obviously proud. The scene was quite a long one, full of Humphrey's inappropriate imagery and tortured rhymes, and of Luce fielding his sorties with clever banter. Dale thought the female love interest was refreshingly intelligent and independent for a Jacobean play.

Eventually Luce agreed readily enough to Humphrey's proposal – with one proviso. "You must be bold, sir. I always swore that no man shall ever enjoy me as his wife unless he steals me hence. If you dare not venture it, sir, then farewell forever!"

Humphrey was equal to the challenge, and promised the use of his pair of Barbary horses for their elopement.

"I am satisfied," Luce declared. "Our course will lie through Waltham forest, where I have a friend who'll welcome us."

She exited, and Humphrey only stayed to declaim one more horrible couplet:

> "I am resolved to venture life and limb
> For one so young, so fair, so kind, so trim."

Nell sighed happily. "Oh My God, Georgie, that is a kind young man, and handsome, and as true as he is tall. If he doesn't win her, it won't be his fault."

"Be patient, mouse. He shall have her, or I'll make some of them pay for it."

"You're a love, Georgie." Nell beamed happily. "He'll be the hero of her life, just like you're the hero of mine."

Georgiana smiled at her young wife with great fond affection, and for a moment the audience was caught in the magic hush –

Until Nell leapt to her feet, crying, "Oh, Georgie, Georgie, now, now, there's Rafe, there's Rafe!"

For at last Rafe was making his entrance through the main doors, with Tim and Frank following him, for the first scene of what would become *The Knight of the Burning Pestle*. The three of them were supposed to all be apprentice grocers, so they were dressed in their regular clothes – shirts, jeans and shoes – each with a grocer's blue apron over the top. Rafe was contemplating an old copy of the chivalric tale *Palmerin of England*, held open in one hand, and Frank seemed lost in wistful thought. Tim still looked peeved, though only mildly so. He carried a broom, which he applied to patches of the stage floor in a desultory manner.

Nell was almost squealing with excitement, despite this quiet tableau.

Georgiana caught her hand, and tugged. "Peace, Nell! Let Rafe alone." But of course as soon as Nell was relatively settled, Georgiana was calling out, "Listen, Rafe, do not strain yourself too much at first. You have a fine voice, if you will not strain it. – Quiet, cony. – In your own time, Rafe."

Rafe began reading out loud from *Palmerin*, picking up the thread mid-tale. "*Then Palmerin and Trineus, snatching their lances from their dwarfs, and clasping their helmets, galloped after the giant. And Palmerin, having gotten a sight of him, spurred on faster, crying, 'Stay, traitorous thief! For thou may not so carry away her who is worth the greatest lord in the world.' And, with these words, Palmerin gave the giant such a blow on the shoulder, that he fell down beside his elephant – and Trineus, coming to the knight who had Agricola behind him, struck the knight off his horse, with his neck broken in the fall – so that the princess Agricola, getting out of the throng, between joy and grief, said, 'Ah, happy knight, the paragon of all who follow arms, now may I be well assured of the love thou bearest me.'*"

Frank was enthralled by the story, and even Tim seemed a little more interested than he really wanted to be.

"I wonder why," Rafe opined, "the kings do not raise an army of fourteen or fifteen hundred thousand men – as big as the army that the Prince of Portugal brought against the heroic Rosicleer – and destroy these giants who do much hurt to wandering damsels, that go in quest of their knights.”

“It’s true,” Nell declared from the audience. “They say no one in Portugal can eat out of doors any more, for the giants and ettins come and snatch their food away.”

“Hush, Nell,” chided her wife. “Go on, Rafe!”

Dale did so, letting Rafe’s earnest dimness carry him through the interruptions unscathed. “Certainly those knights are much to be commended, who leave their everyday lives behind, and wander with a squire and a dwarf through the deserts to relieve poor ladies.”

“Well, Rafe,” said Nell, “I see a lot of ’em walking out on their daily duties, that’s so – but I see precious few relieving us ladies!”

This prompted some wry laughter from the audience.

“There are no such courteous and well-spoken knights in this age,” Rafe continued. “They will call a man ‘the son of a whore’, who Palmerin of England would have called ‘fair sir’ – and a woman who Rosicleer would have called ‘right beauteous damsel’, they will call ‘damned bitch’.”

“That’s true, an’ all! They have called me so a hundred times, and for no good reason.” Nell glared around the audience as if daring anyone to try it.

“But what brave spirit could be content to sit in his shop in a blue apron all day, selling painkillers and bottled water and lottery tickets – when he might pursue feats of arms, and, through his noble achievements, procure a famous history to be written of his heroic prowess?”

“Bravo!” cried Georgiana. “Well said, Rafe. Give us

more of those words!"

"They're fine words," Nell agreed.

"Then why shouldn't I pursue this course, both for the credit of myself and our company? For amongst all the worthy books of achievements, I've never yet read of a grocer-errant." Rafe stood tall, with an easy grace born of an utter lack of guile. "I will be the said knight, and thus I will win the heart of Susan, the fairest maid in London." He looked from one companion to the other. "And have you heard of any that wandered without his squire and his page? My elder prentice Tim shall be my trusty squire, and little Frank shall be my page. Hence, my blue apron!" Rafe cried, matching actions to words and casting his apron aside … "Yet, in remembrance of my former trade, upon my shield shall be portrayed a Burning Pestle, and I will be called the Knight of the Burning Pestle."

Georgiana was nodding in fierce approval. "I knew you wouldn't forget your old trade, Rafe. You're a modest man, and all the sweeter for it."

"Tim!" cried Rafe.

"Yeah?" Tim cleared his throat, and tried for a little more sincerity. "Yes?"

"Tim, my beloved squire, and Frank, my dear dwarf, I charge you that from now on you will ne'er call me by any other name but 'the right courteous and valiant Knight of the Burning Pestle'."

"Uh huh," said Tim – while Frank nodded eagerly.

"And that you never call any woman 'wench', but 'fair lady' if she has her desires, and if not, then 'distressèd damsel'. Also, you will call all forests and heaths 'deserts', and all horses 'palfreys'."

"This is all very fine," Nell said in roundly approving tones. Though she glanced about her at the audience. "Do they like Rafe, do you think, Georgiana?"

"How could they not?" Georgiana complacently replied.

"Now, my beloved squire Tim, if this were a desert, and over it we beheld a knight-errant riding – if I bid you inquire of his intents, what would you say?"

Tim cleared his throat, and addressed the imaginary knight. "Sir, my master sent me to know whither you are riding."

"No, say it thus: 'Fair sir, the right courteous and valiant Knight of the Burning Pestle commanded me to inquire upon what adventure you are bound; whether to relieve some distressèd damsel, or otherwise.' Do you have it?"

Georgiana laughed. "The idiot can't remember all that!"

"It's not like Rafe didn't tell him," muttered Nell, "and twice now."

Tim the squire glared down at them both – and instead, Frank the dwarf stepped forward. "Right courteous and valiant Knight of the Burning Pestle, here is a distressèd damsel who wants to purchase a ha'penny-worth of peppercorns."

Nell and Georgiana burst into a supportive round of applause, with which some of the audience joined in.

"Relieve her, with all courteous language," Rafe loftily commanded. "And now that the fair lady's needs are met, shut up shop. You are no more my prentices, but my trusty squire and dwarf. I must bespeak my shield, emblazoned with a fine sturdy pestle.”

Tim and Frank left the stage – and Rafe was about to follow them when Georgiana spoke.

“Well done, Rafe! You are as good as the best who’ve trod this stage. No – better!”

“Rafe, Rafe!” cried Nell.

He came closer, his posture hunched now into humility. “What is it, mistress?”

“Come back and play another scene soon, sweet Rafe.”

Rafe was too earnest to smile. “As soon as ever I can, fair lady.”

◆

Jasper strode out onto the stage – with his mother, Mistress Merrythought, following along behind trying to keep up with him – for the next scene of *The London Merchant*. An angry glare was directed at Rafe who was only now making a belated exit – and Dale couldn’t help but feel the force of Topher’s impatience in that stare. Mistress Merrythought’s gaze was a little more ambivalent. The actress resented Rafe’s intrusion into their play, of course, but the woman found him quite fanciable.

Rafe cast a last curious glance back over his shoulder as he was disappearing into the darkness of backstage, and saw Jasper turning to Mistress Merrythought, raising his hands in an exasperated prompt.

She took a breath, regathered herself – and then turned on her eldest son, mirroring his exasperation. “Give thee my blessing?! No, and I never will. I’ll see you hanged first! You are your father’s son, Jasper, of the right blood of the

Merrythoughts. I curse the day I met your father. He has spent all his own fortune, and mine, too – and when I tell him of it, he laughs, and dances, and sings, and cries, '*A merry heart lives long-a.*'"

Jasper by now was back in his proper character, listening with humble solemnity to his mother's tirade, but unable to resist a fond smile at this description of his beloved father.

"You are a spendthrift like him," Mistress Merrythought continued, stabbing a finger at him that almost connected with his breastbone. "And now you tell me you've run away from the master who loved you well – and you presume to ask me for help!"

Jasper was about to speak, but Mistress Merrythought swept into her best 'talk to the hand' posture.

"I have nothing for you, Jasper. It's true that I've laid up a little for my Michael, who is his mother's son, but you shan't see a penny of it." She turned away from Jasper and called, "Come here, Michael!"

The younger Merrythought son entered the stage and – in a moment when his mother's attention was elsewhere – pulled a face at his brother. The production had cast the parts with the thought that there was at least five years difference in age between them, or maybe even ten. Michael was still a pampered boy, while Jasper was a young man starting to make his own way in the world.

"Come, Michael," said his mother. "Kneel down, and I shall bless you."

The sanctimonious little twat knelt. "I pray you, mother, pray to God to bless me."

Mistress Merrythought laid her hand upon his head.

"God bless thee, my dear! But Jasper shall never have my blessing; he shall be hanged first. What do you say, Michael?"

"Yes, forsooth, mother, and grace of God."

"That's a good boy!" Mistress Merrythought declared.

"In faith," Nell remarked from the audience, with a complacent nod, "he is a fine-spoken child."

Jasper rolled his eyes at this display from his family and from the Citizens in the audience, but he continued seriously enough, "Mother, it wasn't my choice to leave my master; I didn't run away. And I've not come home to live off you and be idle."

"What an ungracious son the older bloke is!" Nell cried. "Did you hear him, Georgie? How he chops liver with his mother!"

"Chops logic, Nell." Georgiana glowered at Jasper. "But, yes, if he were our son and showed us such disrespect, he'd get short shrift from me."

Jasper was gritting his teeth at these interruptions and insults, and so his delivery of the next line was rather more fraught than it should have been. "I've only come home to ask for your love, mother. I have enough love of my own to marry Luce ten times over, but I'd be a poor man indeed without your love as well."

"You have love enough, you say – and you've caused me sorrow enough, you vagabond! You go in now with Michael, and learn from him what truly matters. I want to have words with your father."

Jasper offered her a half-bow, and accompanied Michael off the stage with a bit of brotherly jostling of elbows. This was the cue for Old Master Merrythought to be heard singing backstage.

Mistress Merrythought looked set to tear her hair out. "There's my husband, singing and carrying on as usual, and I'm left to worry and manage as best I can on nothing at all. – Husband!" she called. "Charles! Charles Merrythought!"

The old man entered, looking cheerfully red-cheeked; in essence, a dishevelled Jacobean Santa Claus. As he continued his song, the musicians in the gallery above joined in with vigour. There was no question at all about where their loyalties lay.

His wife scolded him with hands on hips. "If you considered your state, Charles, you would have little wish to sing."

"I would never consider my state, my estate, or anything else at all, if I thought it would spoil my singing."

"But how will you live, Charles? You're an old man, and cannot work; you have not forty shillings left; and yet you eat good meat, and drink good wine, and you laugh."

"And I'll continue to do so."

"But *how* … ?" she cried in great frustration.

"How? Why, just how I've done it these past forty years! Whenever I came into my dining room, at eleven and six o'clock each day, I found excellent meat and drink on the table. Whenever it looked like my clothes might wear out, next morning a tailor brought me a new suit. Without question it will be so forevermore. But if all should fail, it will take only a little extra effort to laugh myself to death."

Nell was absolutely outraged by this attitude. "Oh. My. God. This old man is the most foolish thing I've ever seen. Is he not, Georgie?"

"You are right, cony."

"You were never imprudent, Georgiana," Nell continued complacently, "and I always loved you for it."

"Aye, cony, we are of one mind."

Old Master Merrythought was considering the Citizens with surprising fondness, while Mistress Merrythought stood there looking outraged.

Finally, once the pair were done with their commentary, Mistress Merrythought continued with a snap in her voice. "Well, Charles, you promised to provide for Jasper, and I have laid up my own treasure for Michael. It's time now to pay Jasper his portion. He has come home. He says his master turned him away, but I don't believe him; I think he ran away. And I will not have the wretch impoverish my Michael."

Nell sprang to her feet. "No, indeed, Mistress Merrythought," she cried reassuringly. "Your older son is a wretch, it's true, but I can promise you that his master *did* turn him away. It all happened right here, in this past half-hour, and it was about the old man's daughter. My wife was here, too, if you won't take my word for it."

Mistress Merrythought's brows were climbing and her

eyes widening in response to this ridiculous claim.

"The boy had served him well enough," Georgiana chimed in, "until the young rogue wanted to marry his master's daughter! But, sweet my wife," she added, reaching to catch Nell's hand in hers, "come sit down. I swear, if there were a thousand boys, you would spoil them all by taking their parts. Let his mother alone with him."

"Yes, Georgie," Nell replied, obediently sitting beside her wife again. "But truth is truth."

Merrythought lavished one last fond look on Nell and Georgiana, and then turned away a little and called out, "Where is Jasper, then? He is always welcome here, but call him in and he shall have his portion. Is he merry?" the old man added.

"Ah, damn him, he is too merry!" his mother complained. "Jasper! Michael!"

The two brothers re-entered the stage, and Michael went to stand by his mother, while Jasper jogged over to enfold his father in a hug which was returned with high interest.

"Welcome, Jasper!" Master Merrythought cried. "Though you've run away from your master's house, I still welcome you. God bless thee! It's your mother's wish that you should receive your portion, and if you're not old enough and wise enough by now to manage it well, then be it on your own head. Hold out your hand!" And Merrythought began counting coins into Jasper's palm. "One, two, three, four, five, six, seven, eight, nine – there is ten shillings for you."

Jasper was initially struck with disappointment, but within a moment a smile dawned, and soon he was grinning as if as appreciative of the joke as anyone else.

"Thrust yourself into the world with that," his father concluded. "Take some settled course – but if fortune crosses thee, come home to me; I still have twenty shillings left."

Jasper thrust the money into his pocket, and listened with affection to his father's advice.

"Be a good and prudent man. Wear ordinary clothes, but eat the best meat, and drink the best drink. Be merry, and give to the poor, and, believe me, you will never want for anything."

"Long may you live free from ill thoughts," Jasper said in return, "and long have cause to be merry!" He took a breath. "But, father –"

"No more words, Jasper," Merrythought replied. "Get thee gone. You have your father's blessing. Farewell, Jasper!

> *"But yet, or ere you part (oh, cruel!)*
> *Kiss me, kiss me, sweeting, mine own dear jewel!*

"So, now begone; no words."

Having pressed his father's hand in his, and bestowed a kiss to his father's round red cheek, Jasper turned and left the stage, much affected by this leave-taking.

"So, Michael," Mistress Merrythought abruptly said, "now get thee gone, too."

"Yes, forsooth, mother; but I'll have my father's blessing first."

"Don't bother, Michael. You don't need his blessing, for you have mine. Begone! I'll fetch my money and jewels, and follow you. I'm leaving your father, too."

A startled wide-eyed Michael turned and fled the stage.

"Truly, Charles, I'll be gone, too."

Old Master Merrythought was, for once, rather shocked by this turn of events. "What! You will not?"

"Indeed I will."

The old man, as was his wont, sang his response:

> *"Heigh-ho, farewell, Nan!*
> *I'll never trust wench more again, if I can."*

"When all your own money is gone, Charles, I won't have you expecting to spend what I've been scraping together for Michael."

"Farewell, good wife! I expect it not. All I have to do in this world is be merry; which I shall, if the ground be not taken from me; and if it be:

> *"When earth and seas from me are reft,*
> *The skies aloft for me are left."*

And the estranged spouses each left the stage, one through the left door and one through the right.

◆

Interlude 1

In the outdoor theatres of Elizabethan and Jacobean times, a play would run straight through, with no intervals. This wasn't possible in indoor theatres, however, as the candles that provided illumination would need trimming. In between the acts, then, there would be a pause in the action on stage, and the musicians would entertain the audience with an instrumental tune, as they had before the play began.

When creating *The Knight of the Burning Pestle*, Francis Beaumont wrote such interludes into the play itself, as the whole thing occurred in 'real time'. Dale wasn't aware of any other play that so perfectly observed the dramatic unities of time and place – and he could argue a case for unity of action, as well, if considered from the Citizens' perspective.

Modern audiences, however, demanded a privy break – and were mostly unfamiliar with the notion of staged interludes – so all this had to be managed very carefully.

◆

As Old Master Merrythought and Mistress Merrythought left the stage through the doors to either side, the Citizens remained firmly seated. Nell turned to Georgiana and loudly declared, "Well, he is a bit of a fool, but he's a merry old gentleman for all that."

The audience shuffled uncertainly, but those who'd read the programme knew to keep their seats, even if they did all look around curiously, unused to such goings-on.

Now the musicians struck up a prancing melody, and Nell leapt to her feet in excitement. "Listen to that, Georgie! Fiddles, real fiddles and fiddlesticks, just like in Ye Olden Times."

Sam stepped out through the main doors, and began a spritely dance to entertain the punters, with much pointing of his toes, and lifting of his rounded arms, and general capering.

"Here's that pretty boy again, Georgie! He has a fine pair of legs on him, don't he?" Nell stood by the edge of the stage, watching appreciatively for a moment or two – but then she turned back to Georgiana and declared, "Sweetheart, we should have Rafe come out and do some of his gambols." She looked around at the audience and assured them, "It would do your hearts good to see him!" before turning back to address Sam: "Thank you, kind youth, that's all very nice – but won't you send Rafe out again?"

Sam lost his rhythm in consternation, and sagged a little.

Georgiana stood up and went for the kill. "Sirrah, you scurvy boy, go back and tell the players to send Rafe, or, by God's wounds, I'll come back there and tear off their wigs. This is all stuff and nonsense!"

The musicians had already ended on a mangled chord. Sam whimpered and fled from the stage.

◆

Backstage

As Venturewell and Humphrey bustled out to begin Act Two a little sooner than planned, Dale found himself confronted by Topher in the green room. Well. Not that Topher was actually doing the confronting. Not that Topher was doing anything remotely related to Dale at all.

In truth, he was down the far end of the room, kneeling before their Old Master Merrythought, who was sitting slumped back on one of the sagging grey sofas – and Topher was massaging one of the old man's calves.

When Merrythought saw Dale watching them, he called, "Nothing peculiar going on, I promise! This lad was kind enough to take pity on my cramping calf muscles, that's all. I love this place, but the staircases don't love me."

Topher smiled up at Merrythought as his hands continued working patiently, rhythmically; and Dale couldn't help but soften a little into affection. Topher had such a knack for helping others, and for doing so with an easy grace, that Dale felt quite clueless and clumsy in comparison. He tried to focus on that now and build up some resentment, but Dale merely ended up feeling fond. It was hard work to dislike Topher, and even Dale had observed that no one else seemed to bother.

"It's the Winter Solstice tonight," Merrythought was continuing, apparently apropos of nothing much. "The longest night of the year. The world makes its great turn from dark towards light, and we shed the old and start our journey towards the new. There ..." He fell into a contemplative silence for a few moments, before finally stirring and saying to Topher, "There, that's enough now. You're a good lad, Topher."

"Not a problem," said Topher, standing up and dusting off his hands as if pleased by a job well done. "Glad to help."

Through all that, Dale had been standing stranded by the rack of costumes, due to put on his knightly gear for his next scene – but he'd barely managed to locate his chainmail tunic, let alone take it down from the rack.

Topher now wandered over, and as he drew closer – gazing steadily at Dale all the while – his mouth took on a sour twist.

"What's up?" Dale found himself asking. Then he grimaced, mentally kicking himself. He knew better than to give the guy an inch, if Topher wanted to take an emotional mile.

Topher shrugged, and collapsed down onto the sofa placed next to the costumes.

"You know it's the last –"

"You remember the last –"

They'd each spoken and then crunched to a halt in jangling unison. Glares ricocheted off each other. The warmth and quiet generated by Merrythought, and by Topher's kindness to him, was already forgotten.

Silence for a moment, and then Topher asked in perfectly-tuned snide tones, "How's the Life Plan coming along? All working out nicely, is it?"

Dale glanced across at the others, but even Merrythought was safely oblivious. Topher and Dale were being quiet enough to not draw attention, despite the tension between them ramping up to eleven. So Dale gritted out, "What the actual *fuck*, Topher?"

"You know, that Grand Life Plan of yours, that has no room in it for … for … *dating* or anything." Topher glanced away, obviously conscious of ineloquence.

"For fuck's sake," Dale grumbled, "who *dates* any more?"

"Not you, that's for sure! Do you have any friends left, Dale? I bet you can't even fit *friends* into your schedule, let alone anything else!"

Anger spiked through him again. "Fuck off, Topher! I have *friends*," Dale insisted with a hiss – before turning away and grabbing Rafe's heavy chainmail off its hanger. He started clumsily struggling into it, but was too incensed to ask for help.

When Dale's head emerged again and the chainmail tunic settled heavily onto his shoulders, he saw that Topher was still sitting there, almost literally chewing over a number of retorts. Dale huffed, and reached for Rafe's belt and baldric to buckle on.

Finally Topher said, "And your much-vaunted career? Going well, is it?"

Dale quite inadvertently smiled at that, and tipped a sardonic wink at Topher. "Back-to-back jobs this whole year, and I worked with Ian McKellen, if you remember, *and* Ang Lee."

"It was only a short for charity!"

"Like you're not jealous," Dale sniped.

"Yet here you are," Topher returned in tones as heavy as fate, "back where you started, in the same show as me."

"At least I'm the *lead*."

"Oh no, you're not. The Citizens are."

Dale grabbed up his sword and helmet, and turned away towards the corridor that led to the stage. But then he turned back, and he leaned in to hiss, "The work always comes first. I'm not gonna apologise for that. You see where it takes me, and try not to drown in the envy."

"Oh yeah, sure," Topher lightly replied. "And you try not to drown in the lonely."

They stared at each other, both venomous and hurting.

The sound system crackled into life, and the Stage Manager asked, "Dale, are you ready? Rafe is on in a few."

Dale straightened up, and lifted the helmet in acknowledgement towards the CCTV camera up in the corner of the room. Then he turned and strode away, taking deep breaths, and forcing himself to remember Rafe's earnest equanimity.

The work came first, and the show must go on, and all that – no matter how deeply annoying one's colleagues were.

◆

Act Two

Venturewell wanted to know how Humphrey's proposal to Luce had gone – and Humphrey addressed him, of course, in a rhyming couplet:

> "Right worshipful, and my beloved friend
> And father dear, this matter's at an end."

"I'm glad the girl was so tractable," her father remarked in surprise.

But then Humphrey began laboriously explaining that actually Luce had challenged Humphrey to steal her away from home before dawn the next day. Which, after all, was not the kind of thing most fathers would be glad to hear.

"Georgie," cried Nell, "do you think it will be a match? Tell me what you think, my sweet rogue. You see how the poor young gentleman is so anxious about it. – Be at rest, good sir! I'll come up there and convince her father myself."

"No, sit down, honeysuckle," said her wife. "If the father denies him, I'll call half-a-dozen of our finest fellows to come by, and they can do any convincing that's needed."

"I could kiss you for that, Georgie! Oh, I bet you were a devil in your day, my dearest, but God forgive you, as I do with all my heart."

Venturewell and Humphrey had listened to all this in growing alarm, not to mention confusion. Finally, when it seemed that Nell was done for now, Venturewell turned to Humphrey. "Where were we? Oh, I have it: You told me that tomorrow before daybreak you must convey her hence."

"I must, I must; and thus it is agreed:
Your daughter rides upon a brown-bay steed,
I on a sorrel, which I bought of Brian,
The honest host of the roaring Red Lion,
In wild Waltham forest. So, if you may,
Consent here and now, and do not delay."

"You know," said her father, "I'll willingly agree to anything you want, if it's good and fair. Steal her when you will, if that brings pleasure to you both, and I promise I'll sleep through it, to help bring you joy." Venturewell let out a sigh, though. "But tell me why you cannot perform your marriage safely here at home … ?"

"Aw, bless you, old man!" called Nell. "You don't want to part these two true hearts, do you? This fine young man has her, Georgie, and I'm right glad. … Georgie? Why aren't you happy?"

"Once Rafe comes out again, I'll be as merry as you like, my wife."

Humphrey cleared his throat, and began a long and winding explanation of Luce's oath.

"… And yet why did she swear?
Truly, I cannot tell, unless it were
For her own ease; for, sure, sometimes an oath,
Being sworn thereafter, is like cordial broth."

And so he meandered on, until Venturewell was at last reassured. "If this is all, you need not fear any denials to your love. Proceed; I'll neither follow, nor repent the deed."

Humphrey, of course, was delighted.

> "Good night, twenty good nights, and twenty more,
> And twenty more good nights – that makes three score!"

◆

As Venturewell and Humphrey left the stage, Sam entered with a dancer's step and pointed toes, and hung a new board below the one announcing 'The London Merchant'. This one read 'Waltham Forest'. Sam performed his best arm-flourish to draw attention to it. And then he scrammed before the Citizens could detain him for questioning.

Out came Mistress Merrythought, with a shiny casket under one arm and a leather purse in her hand, looking about her warily at the dark forest. Michael followed her, oblivious to the dangers due to a complete lack of imagination.

"Come, Michael," said Mistress Merrythought at last. "Are you not tired, boy?"

"No, forsooth, mother, not I."

"Where are we, do you know?"

"Indeed, forsooth, mother, I cannot tell, unless we be at Mile-End. … Is not all the world Mile-End, mother?"

This earned a scattering of enthusiastic applause and a

hearty cheer from the audience.

"No, Michael, not all the world, boy."

"Mother, forsooth. Shall not my father come with us?"

"No, Michael, let your father go hang himself. I am done with him. Let him stay at home, and sing for his supper." After a moment, though, she smiled at her son and softened a little. "Come, child, sit down, and I'll show you fine trinkets, indeed."

They sat together towards the front of the stage, and Mistress Merrythought put the casket between them and opened it up. "Look here, Michael; here's a ring, and here's a brooch, and here's a bracelet, and here's two rings more." She opened up the leather purse and propped it by the casket. "And here's money and gold aplenty, my boy."

"Shall I have all this, mother?"

"Aye, Michael, you shall have it all."

Georgiana had been sitting there impatiently with her arms crossed. "How do you like this, wench?" she asked Nell.

"I don't know," Nell replied. "I would have Rafe out here again, Georgie. I couldn't be bothered watching anything else, with all this fine 'forsooth this' and 'forsooth that'!"

Which was when Rafe made a timely entrance, with squire Tim and dwarf Frank at his shoulders. Mistress Merrythought and Michael froze, and stared in bafflement at these intruders.

"Here's Rafe at last!" cried Georgiana.

"How do you do, Rafe?" Nell asked. "You are *so* welcome, I can't even! Now, hold up your head, and go to it with gusto, and everyone here will love you like I do."

Mistress Merrythought shifted uneasily, as if uncertain how to deal with this hijacking of her scene.

"My trusty squire," Rafe began, "unlace my helm, and give me my hat. Where are we? What desert may this be?"

"Mirror of knighthood," Frank replied – "oh, Shining Example of knighthood – this is, as I take it, the perilous Waltham-down, in whose bottom stands the enchanted valley."

Mistress Merrythought decided that discretion was the better part of valour. "Oh, Michael, we are betrayed!" she cried, jumping to her feet. "We are betrayed! Here be giants! Fly, boy, fly!" And the two of them carefully circled around out of reach of the knight and his attendants, before dashing out through the main door at the back of the stage.

Rafe watched them go, and then ordered, "Lace on my helm again. What noise is this? A gentle lady, fleeing the embrace of some uncourteous knight! I will rescue her. Go, squire, and say that the Knight who wears this Pestle in honour of fair Susan and of all ladies, swears revenge upon the traitorous coward who pursues her. Go, comfort her, and that gentle squire who bears her company."

Tim managed to declare a half-hearted "I go, brave knight", before exiting.

"My trusty dwarf and friend," Rafe continued, "reach me my shield, and hold it while I swear. First, by my knighthood; then by the soul of Amadis de Gaul, my famous ancestor; then by my sword that the beauteous Brionella girt about me." Rafe struck an even taller, nobler pose.

Frank produced a gold-painted Pestle, and held it aloft

with a reverent flourish.

"And by this bright burning Pestle, of mine honour the living trophy." Rafe took the Pestle from Frank, and thrust it into his belt. "And by all respect due to distressèd damsels. ... Here I vow never to end the quest of this fair lady and that forsaken squire till by my valour I gain their liberty!"

The little man echoed his noble pose, and declared, "Heaven bless the knight who thus relieves poor errant gentlewomen!"

Rafe and Frank exited the stage, to Nell's distress. "That was great! That was so effing good! But, Georgie, I won't have him leaving again so soon. Call Rafe back again, Georgie! Let him come fight before me, and let's have some drums and some trumpets, and let him kill all that come near him. Call him back, if you love me, Georgie!"

"Peace a little, sweetheart," said Georgiana. "He shall have his chance, and he shall kill them all, even if there were twenty more of them than there are."

Now the lone Jasper ventured forth into the forest, addressing the goddess of Fortune. "Show me your generous face, oh Fortuna; turn your wheel and let me rise again, let me stand." He looked about him. "This is where Luce agreed to meet me, if love has any constancy. Oh, these days, only wealthy men are counted as happy! So how shall I please thee, Fortuna, when I am only rich in misery? My father's blessing and these few coins are my inheritance." Jasper shook his head over the ten shillings in his palm. "Well, from earth thou art, and to the earth I give thee." He threw the money across the forest floor, into the back corner of the stage. "There grow and multiply, while fresher air breeds me a fresher fortune."

After a moment's reflection he turned around – and did a double-take. "Is this an illusion?" Jasper approached the abandoned casket and purse. "Is this some devilry?" He warily picked up and checked over the treasure. "No, it's real, it rings true. I am not dreaming! Oh, God's dear blessing upon the heart of him that left it here! It's mine. These pearls were not left for swine."

And so Jasper exited a happier and much richer man.

Nell, of course, was unimpressed. "I do not like that this unthrifty youth should steal away the money. The poor gentlewoman, his mother, will have a heavy heart for losing it, god knows."

"With good reason, sweetheart," Georgiana agreed.

"But let him go for now. I'll tell Rafe about it, and he'll fetch the rascal back again with a vengeance, if he be not dead. Anyway, Georgie," she added, gesturing around at the audience nearby, "here are a number of ladies and gentlemen who can witness his thievery, and myself, and yourself, and the musicians, if we be called in question." Nell was distracted from such serious matters by the entrance of the Knight and his dwarf. "Here comes Rafe, Georgie! Now we shall hear him speak as if he were an empor- … an empor- … warrior."

Georgiana cast her a ruefully fond look.

Rafe asked, "Has my squire not returned?"

"Right courteous knight," Frank replied, "your squire doth come, and with him comes the lady and her companion."

Tim – still looking much put-upon – entered, along

with a nervous Mistress Merrythought, handkerchief in hand, and a confused Michael.

Rafe struck a noble pose. "Madam, if any service of a poor errant knight may right your wrongs, command it. I am ready to give you succour; for to that holy end I bear my armour."

"Alas, sir, I am a poor gentlewoman," Mistress Merrythought replied, dabbing at a tear or two on her cheek, "and I have lost all my money in this forest!"

"Rather 'desert', you would say, lady – and not 'lost' while I have sword and lance. Dry up your tears, which ill befit the beauty of that face, and tell the story of your disastrous fortune."

Mistress Merrythought's spirits were most happily revived by Rafe's gallantry. "Yes, alas! I left a … a thousand pound, yes, a thousand pound – all the money I had put by for this youth – upon seeing you emerge from the dark forest … the, uh, dark desert. But you looked so grim! And, forgive me, more like a giant than a mortal man."

"I am as you are, lady," Rafe assured her, before indicating his companions, "and so are they; all mortal." He turned his attentions to Michael. "But why weeps this gentle squire?"

"Has he not cause to weep, do you not think, when he has lost his inheritance?"

Rafe stood tall again. "Young Hope of Valour, weep not! I will confound thy foe, who dares to deny equity to distressèd squires and ladies. I have but one horse," Rafe continued, indicating an imaginary mount, "on which shall ride this fair lady and this courteous squire."

Mistress Merrythought and Michael stared blankly at the invisible horse, but, after a moment, Mistress Merrythought took Michael by the hand and tugged him forward to take their places in the assemblage. She cast a game smile at Rafe.

"Fortune will give us more upon our next adventure!" Rafe declared. "Come trot beside us, squire and dwarf, to do us need."

Exeunt the adventurers!

Dale had to admit that he enjoyed these parts best, where the story of *The London Merchant* and *The Knight of the Burning Pestle* interwove, and the disgruntled wife found solace in the innocent knight.

◆

"Did not I tell you, Nell," said Georgiana, "what your man would do? By the faith of my body, wench, for clever action and good delivery, the others on this stage may all cast their caps at him."

"And so they may, Georgie. If Rafe is not stolen away this night by some company of players, I shall eat my hat." Nell patted her hair, and laughed. "Well, I shall eat someone's hat! But if they do take him, Georgie, we must not repent. We have done our parts, and I'm sure Rafe will have the grace to be thankful."

"I warrant he will, duckling."

◆

The eloping pair, Humphrey and Luce, now entered what

was supposed to be 'another part of the forest'. The suitor
was in as fine a rhyming form as ever.

> "Good Mistress Luce, however I in fault am
> For your lame horse, you're welcome unto
>   Waltham.
> But which way now to go, or what to say,
> I know not truly, till it be broad day."

Luce was entirely capable of dealing with the challenges
herself, however. "Fear not, Master Humphrey. I am a
good enough guide for this place."

Humphrey politely and clumsily invited her, "if it
please you," to ride or walk, or sit or "go pluck a rose" –
which meant to take a comfort break, though Dale was
sure that few if any of the audience would realise just how
clueless Humphrey could be –

> "Any of which shall be indifferent
> To your good friend Humphrey, whose consent
> Is so entangled ever to your will,
> As the poor harmless horse is to the mill."

"Say the word," said Luce, "and we'll sit down, and take
a nap."

"And one of us keep a watch," Humphrey fretted,
looking about him. "If we were still in the town, we might
both nap together."

"You're merry, Master Humphrey!" she mock-scolded.

"Why, so I am."

Which was when Jasper caught up with them, and ran

up crying, "Luce! My dear friend Luce!"

"My own Jasper."

"I am yours, as you are mine," he declared, taking her in his arms.

Luce happily returned the embrace – watched by Humphrey, whose shock was already turning bitter. It was almost heart-breaking to watch, for Jeremy played Humphrey's hurt as real and deeply felt, below all the bluster.

"If it be so, my friend," said Humphrey, "you use me ill. What do you think I am?"

"An arrant simpleton," Jasper retorted.

"A true insult for a gentleman!" Recognition had sparked in Humphrey's eyes – and he drew his sword. "And you're but a prentice. Now, by God's body, I'll tell thy master; for I know thee well."

Jasper, who was armed with only a dagger, looked about him for anything that would serve as a longer weapon or a shield, but there was nothing on the empty stage. "Will you be so forward for to tell?" Jasper ducked and rushed his rival, getting in under Humphrey's sword arm before the fellow knew quite what he was about. "Take that," Jasper cried, pummelling him across the back of his shoulders with the dagger-hilt in his fist, and beating him down to the ground, though not letting his blows land too hard. "And take that – and tell my master, sir, that I gave it, and say, I paid you well."

Humphrey collapsed towards the front of the stage, pressing a hand to his heart as if that was what caused him most pain. "Oh, sir, I have your message and do confess the payment! Pray, withdraw."

Having won the game, set and match, Jasper stepped back towards Luce, while still addressing Humphrey. "Go, sir, get you to your night-cap and the nourishment to cure your beaten bones."

"Alas, poor Humphrey," said Luce, with enough genuine sympathy to rekindle a sad light in Humphrey's eyes. "Get thee some wholesome broth, with sage and comfrey – and a little oil of roses and someone with a gentle touch to anoint thy back."

"What a fool I have been," he complained.

"Farewell, my pretty Nump," said Luce. "I am very sorry I cannot bear thee company."

"Farewell," Humphrey replied as Luce and Jasper exited the stage. Then he muttered disconsolately, "The devil's dame was ne'er so banged in Hell."

Nell was on her feet in outrage. "This Jasper bloke is out of control! Georgie, do you see how he swaggers about, and flies at people as if he were a fire-breathing dragon? What a knave! If I don't teach him a lesson for hurting this poor gentleman, I am no true woman. His friends have done him wrong, if they've indulged him in his spiteful humours. He'll end up on the gallows!"

"You're too bitter, cony," said Georgiana. "The fellow may do well enough for all this. You know we've both seen worse young men come good again."

Nell grabbed up her handbag, and went to stand as close to where Humphrey lay as she could. "Come closer, Master Humphrey, if you can. Has he hurt you? Fie upon his fists for those blows he dealt you! Here, sweetheart," she added, reaching for a packet in her bag, "here's some green ginger to chew on. Not that the young strumpet was wrong, with her sage and her comfrey, and you can buy them in goodly quantities at any of Georgiana's shops, but …" Nell had been soothingly stroking Humphrey's hair, and now gasped. "Heaven help me, he has a lump on his head from when he fell, as big as an ostrich's egg! Aw, you poor sweet lamb, how your temples beat!" She turned back to Georgie, and implored, "You'll talk to the police, won't you, sweetheart? That Jasper needs to be bound up – or tied down, or whatever it is – to keep the peace!"

"I'll do better than that," Georgiana replied, standing up to pace at the foot of the stage. "I'll have Rafe fight with him, and beat him six ways from Sunday." She called towards the tiring house, "Sirrah – boy – come out here!"

Sam appeared, and edged towards Georgiana, casting a nervous glance at Humphrey, who remained lying there on the stage accepting Nell's attentions. Was Jeremy simply trying to stay in character, Sam seemed to be pondering, or had they all just given up at this point?

"Let Rafe come in and fight with Jasper," Georgiana demanded.

Sam took a step back in shock. "You're not serious."

"We are, too," Nell declared. "And let Rafe beat him well. That Jasper needs to be taught what's what."

Sam lifted his hands with his palms out placatingly. "Good madam grocer, you must excuse us. Our play is a romantic comedy, and the most it can encompass is a couple of blows with little harm done –"

"Oi!" protested Humphrey.

"– but if we tried to include a big fight scene, it would spoil the plot."

"Plot me no plots!" cried Georgiana. "I'll have Rafe

come out now, and Jasper, too – or I'll make your house too hot for you!"

"Well, madam, then he shall. But if our story goes awry, the audience must forgive us."

"Go your ways, then, my good lad!" Georgiana strutted along in front of the stage, mighty pleased with herself. "I'll bet him a tenner, that boy shall have his bellyful of fighting now. Oh, and now here comes Rafe!"

◆

The Knight of the Burning Pestle entered, along with Mistress Merrythought and Michael, his squire Tim and his dwarf Frank. They were hardly onto the stage before they noticed Humphrey, still gamely lying there where he was felled.

Rafe brought his party to a halt. "What knight is that, squire? Ask him if he is guarding this place, bound by the love of a lady fair, or if he is on an adventure."

"Sir, I am no knight," Humphrey replied, as he used Tim's support to help drag himself up to his feet, "but a poor gentleman, who has had stolen from me, this very night, my lovely fiancée. The miscreant was not content with that, but must leave me bruises to remind me of my loss."

"Aye, Rafe," Nell called, sitting on the edge of her seat. "He beat this fine gent unmercifully. Do not spare him, Rafe. Do not spare him!"

"Hush, wife, no more. No more."

Rafe stepped forward, visibly taking upon him this task. "Where is the wretch that hath done this deed?" He turned back to address Mistress Merrythought. "Your pardon, lady, if you will, so that I may pursue this wicked knight? And thou, fair young squire: you will understand if I put aside the great venture of the purse and the rich casket, until I have completed this other quest?"

They each nodded enthusiastically, quite enamoured by now of the Knight and his adventures.

Humphrey staggered a pace, clutching hard at Tim's shoulder. "Here comes the cad who purloined my treasure!"

Jasper and Luce entered hand in hand, and the small stage began to feel a bit crowded, while the energies ratcheted up a notch. On seeing Rafe, Jasper's expression turned cold.

Rafe cleared his throat, betraying a slight falter in his sense of purpose for the first time. "Go, squire, and tell him that I am here, an errant knight-at-arms, to demand delivery of that fair lady to her own knight's arms."

"Are you *sure*?" asked Tim, not even bothering to lower his voice. "He'll have you for breakfast!"

Rafe pulled himself up taller, and tried to ignore these doubts. "If he denies you, squire, bid him to take his choice of ground, and so defy him."

Tim let out a sigh, and then trudged over to face Jasper. "From the Knight that bears the Golden Pestle, I defy thee, knight, unless you make fair restitution of that bright lady."

Jasper defied him right back – and Topher delivered Jasper's glare at Rafe with a little more fire than Dale felt was strictly warranted. Jasper wound his arm firm around Luce's waist, and retorted, "Tell the knight that sent thee, he is an *ass*, and I will keep the wench, and knock off his helmet."

"Knight," cried Rafe in ringing tones, "thou art but dead, if thou recall not thy uncourteous terms."

Nell burst up onto her feet. "Break his head, Rafe! Break his head, Rafe, and soundly, too!"

"Come, knight," cried Jasper, letting go of Luce in order to beckon Rafe forward with both hands, "I am ready for you."

Rafe gamely took a step towards Jasper, though the grocer's apprentice was obviously feeling a bit wary, and almost visibly reminding himself that this was, after all, only stage-fighting. Dale suspected the unnerving flint in Jasper's hard stare was partly inspired by Topher's anger at Dale himself.

Jasper leapt forward, and grabbed the Pestle from Rafe's belt. "Now your pestle shall test the mettle of your mortar!" With his hand wrapped around the Pestle, Jasper swung a right hook into Rafe's jaw. *Whack!* came the sound effects from backstage.

Rafe spun around a full three-sixty degrees, and wavered there, stunned but still upright.

"With that," Jasper said, narrating as if he himself were a knight in one of Palmerin's tales, "he stood upright in his stirrups, and gave the Knight of the Peppercorn such a knock –" Jasper rose up, and clouted Rafe over his helmeted head. *Thunk!*

The other characters on stage all gasped. Mistress Merrythought and Frank seemed genuinely distraught. Humphrey and Luce were terrified. Tim was gaping in shock – and he also looked truly involved for the first time.

Rafe fell down as if his sinews had momentarily turned to jelly. Dale wasn't having to act very much at this point.

"– such a great knock that he forsook his horse," Jasper continued, "and down the Knight fell." Jasper stood over Rafe triumphantly. "And then he leaped upon him, and plucking off his helmet –" Jasper matched actions to words, snatching off Rafe's helm. He lifted the Pestle for the killing blow, roaring out an inarticulate battle cry –

"Nay," said Humphrey, "if the noble knight who avenges me is down so soon, then though I can scarcely walk, I needs must run." And Humphrey quickly hobbled out through the nearest door, the one to the right.

Jasper watched him go in consternation, and turned to Luce as if disturbed that in her distress she would be so easily deserted by any man, let alone by one who'd pledged himself to her.

Tim and Frank had taken the opportunity of Jasper's distraction to grab Rafe by the heels and drag him out from under Jasper. They helped the groggy Rafe to his feet, though he leaned on them heavily.

"Run, Rafe!" called Nell. "Run, Rafe – run for your life!"

The Knight, his squire and his dwarf made their way as fast as they could through the door on the left.

"Jasper comes, Jasper comes!" Nell warned them.

But Jasper did not follow them. Instead he stood, and took a breath, and carelessly tossed away the Pestle.

Mistress Merrythought scurried across to pick up the precious Pestle, and then she and Michael supported each other arm-in-arm as they exited the stage together, following the Knight and his party, and casting nervous glances back at Jasper.

But Jasper ignored them, too. Taking his love into a warm embrace, Jasper said, "Come, Luce, come. We must look after you. Humphrey, and Golden Pestle, both adieu!"

And the two lovers left the stage in each other's embrace, through the main door.

◆

Backstage, Topher was waiting for Dale, as he always did after the fight scene. He held out his hand in greeting, in the same way that opponents on a sports field would shake hands after a match. "No harm done?" Topher murmured. Not that actors ever wanted to really hurt each other during such scenes, but by his nature Topher was more concerned than most.

Dale grasped his hand, and answered, as he always did, "No harm at all." Then he pursed his lips in amusement and added, "Don't tell me you didn't enjoy that, though!"

After a moment, Topher slowly grinned at him, as if appreciating the joke. "Maybe a bit," he admitted. And it was true that Topher seemed a little more relaxed and happy again, as if he'd needed to let off a little steam. Maybe it was the case that Dale looked rather more centred, too, or maybe despite himself he betrayed a slight crackle of desire. Because in the next moment, without letting go of Dale's hand, Topher took a step forward – and brushed a dry kiss across Dale's lips. It wasn't the most passionate of kisses. It could have been interpreted as merely friendly. But it was a kiss.

"No real harm done?" Topher asked again, close enough that they were sharing their breath.

"Not yet!" Dale replied, tightening his grasp, and revelling in the strong, competent grip and the tender, smooth skin of Topher's hand. Something daring surged up within Dale and almost surfaced. He wondered if Topher would read the message in the smile that involuntarily quirked Dale's lips: *Not yet, no – so do keep trying.* Sometimes a man needed to be challenged, after all. Sometimes he *wanted* to be convinced, and his better judgement be damned.

Topher nodded somewhat enigmatically and stepped away. Dale stood there almost swaying with warmth, and the air where Topher had been was startlingly cool on his skin. Then Topher took another step, and vanished into the dimness of backstage – and Dale was alone.

◆

Nell was on her feet again, leaning back against the stage and looking mighty peeved. "Surely the devil (God bless us!) is in this youth Jasper! Georgie, did you ever see such a dragon? He hit Rafe so hard, I'm afraid my boy might catch his death from a concussion. If my Rafe dies – then, even though Jasper was Old Master Merrythought's son a thousand times over, if there is any law in England, I'll make them pay for it."

Georgie snorted, and got up to stand beside her wife, arms firmly crossed. "No, I have worked it out, sweetheart. Weren't you watching? Our Rafe didn't even land one blow. It's as if he were paralysed. So, as sure as we stand here, that Jasper is enchanted. All else being equal, he could no more have stood in Rafe's hands than I could in my Lord Mayor's. I'll have from them a ring to discover all enchantments, and Rafe shall beat that Jasper yet. Don't fret about it, Nell, for it shall be so."

A moment of hush passed with the Citizens deep in pensive thought.

And then Rafe poked his head around the doorframe through which he'd exited, and cautiously looked about to see what was what.

The audience laughed in reaction, and the Citizens turned around to see what was going on. "Oh, wife, here's Rafe again!"

Frank the dwarf poked his head out – somewhat below Rafe as befitted their relative heights – and looked about the stage.

And then Tim the squire poked his head out, too – somewhat below Frank, almost at floor level.

The audience were cracking up badly, for this joke never got old, but Rafe and his sidekicks played it completely straight-faced. One by one they popped out of sight again – and then after a moment, reassured that Jasper had withdrawn from the field of battle, our three heroes carefully emerged onto the stage, stepping silently across the wooden boards.

When they were all three well out in plain sight, Tim accidentally dropped Rafe's helmet, which fell with such a loud clang that Frank and Rafe turned and leapt about like frightened cats. *Sorry*, Tim silently mouthed, *sorry* – and they each gestured soothingly at the others as if to convey, *It's all right, it's all right, calm down.*

Then, once the three of them had again reassured themselves that they were alone on the stage, they each relaxed and stood a little taller. Tim hissed back towards the door, and beckoned. Mistress Merrythought and Michael warily joined them.

Rafe cleared his throat, and was just about to speak –

"Stay, Rafe, wait," commanded Nell. "Let me speak with you. How are you, Rafe? Are you badly hurt? That great foul lout has no mercy in his soul!" Nell rummaged in her handbag. "Here's some candy for you, sweet Rafe. And now you go on. You shall have another bout with that Jasper, and it will all fall out very differently this time!"

Rafe looked a bit taken aback at the thought of having to go through the fight again, but he put on a brave enough face.

Georgiana had sat back down again, with her arms still firmly crossed. "If not here, then Rafe shall have him at the fencing-school – and if he does not make a coward out of that Jasper, and drive him up and down the room, he shall never come back to work in my shop."

Rafe gulped.

Mistress Merrythought – still bearing the Pestle in both hands, and unable to keep from absentmindedly fondling it – now bustled forward to try to change the uncomfortable subject. "Truly, Master Knight of the Burning Pestle, I am weary."

"Indeed, forsooth, mother," said Michael, "and I am very hungry."

Rafe swept out a magnanimous hand. "Take comfort, gentle dame, and you, fair squire, for in this desert there must needs be placed many strong castles, held by courteous knights." He carefully took the Pestle from Mistress Merrythought's hands, and brandished it. "Till I bring you safe to one of those, I swear by this my order of knighthood never to leave you."

"Well said, Rafe!" Nell cried, as the Knight thrust the Pestle back into his belt where it belonged. "Well said! Georgie, Rafe was always helpful, was he not? And if he could not help, he would always sooth you with fine words."

"Yes, duck."

"I shall never forget him, in all my life. When he had lost our child, our daughter Apple – and we named her so for she was ever as crisp and fresh and delicious as an autumn apple – When he had lost our child in the markets, she strayed all the way to Puddle Wharf by herself, and we had the whole neighbourhood out calling for her – 'Apple! Sweet Apple!' – And there at the docks she would have drowned herself in our mighty Thames, if it weren't for a boatman hauling her out." Nell nodded to herself, as tranquil now as she'd been frightened then. "And all that morning, Rafe was the most help and comfort to me: 'Peace, mistress,' says he, 'let it go. I'll get you another as good.' Did he not, Georgie? Did he not say so?"

"Yes, indeed he did, mouse," Georgiana equably agreed.

A respectful hush swelled within the room.

And then, judging the timing to a nicety, Frank the dwarf finally stepped forward, and the audience's focus returned to the adventurers on the stage.

"I wish," Frank said to Tim the squire, "that we had a

bowl of stew and a pot of ale, my friend, and then were going to bed!"

"Why," said Tim, looking about and reimagining the stage according to their needs, "and soon we shall. We are at the edge of Waltham town, and that's the Bell Inn."

Frank broke into happy verse.

> "Take courage, valiant knight, damsel, and squire!
> I have discovered, not a stone's throw off,
> An ancient castle, held by the old knight
> Of the most holy order of the Bell,
> Who welcomes all knights-errant.
> There plenty is of food, and all prepared
> By the white hands of his own lady dear."

His companions were grinning and nodding, and obviously thought this was excellent stuff, so Frank continued.

> "He has three squires who greet all his guests.
> The first, called Chamberlino, who will see
> Our beds prepared, and bring us snowy sheets,
> On which ne'er prentice placed his muddy feet.
> The second, called Tapstero, who will see
> Our ale pots filled, and no froth therein.
> The third, a gentle squire, Ostlero called,
> Who will our palfreys groom with wisps of straw,
> And in the manger give them oats aplenty,
> And never grease their teeth with candle-wax."

Nell led a hearty round of applause. "That dwarf is a fine fellow," she told anyone in hearing distance, "though if you ask me, the squire's a bit of a muppet."

Rafe loftily ignored this, and commanded, "Knock at the gates, my squire, with stately lance."

Well, Tim didn't have a lance to hand, so he shrugged and headed over to the door on the left at the back of the stage, and knocked three times – jumping as his blows were exaggerated by sound effects from backstage. *Thud! Thud! Thud!*

The tapster entered the stage, tankard and cloth in his hands, crying, "Who's there?" He only took a moment to size up the party. "You are welcome, my lady, and all you gentlemen. Will you see a room?"

Frank undertook the introductions. "Right courteous and valiant Knight of the Burning Pestle, this is the Squire Tapstero."

"Fair Squire Tapstero," said Rafe, "I am a wandering knight, of the order of the Burning Pestle, in the quest of this fair lady's casket and purse. Losing myself in this vast wilderness, I am to this castle well by fortune brought – where, hearing of the goodly hospitality that your knight of the holy order of the Bell gives to all damsels and errant knights, I thought to knock, and now am bold to enter."

The tapster let this all fly past him with a dazed look on his face. Once a silence stretched long enough for him to be sure that Rafe was done, the tapster said, "Yeah, all right." Then he cleared his throat and rephrased his original offer somewhat. "If it please you to see a chamber, sir, you are very welcome."

"Thank you," said Rafe. And the Knight and his party

followed the tapster through into the inn (that is, backstage).

◆

After a moment, Sam carefully poked his head out through the middle door. The Citizens both seemed safely caught up in their own pensive thoughts – so, keeping as much of himself as possible behind the door and its curtain, Sam reached a long arm for the board marked 'Waltham Forest'. The audience watched with hushed breath as he managed to free it from its hangings with one hand. Once he was done, he drew it in past the curtain – let out a relieved sigh when he realised he hadn't yet been observed – and then slipped back within the tiring house himself.

◆

"Georgie," said Nell disconsolately, "I would have something done, and I cannot tell you what it is."

"Speak your mind, Nell," said her wife.

"Why, Georgie, shall Rafe beat nobody again? Sweetheart, do please let him."

"So he shall, Nell – and if I join with him, we'll beat them all."

Humphrey and Venturewell now entered the stage.

"Oh, Georgie, here's Master Humphrey again, who lost his darling Luce, and here's Miss Luce's father. Master Humphrey will do something heroic, I am sure of it."

When Nell was quiet again, Humphrey could no longer

delay breaking the bad news to Venturewell:

> "Father, it's true in arms I ne'er shall clasp 'er;
> For she is stolen away by your man Jasper."

"I thought he would tell him," Nell said complacently, as the audience chortled away at Humphrey's awful rhyming.

Venturewell was unimpressed. "What an unhappy man am I, to lose my child! I remember Jasper telling me what a fool you are, and now I begin to give him credence. Why did you let her go? If you loved her, you wouldn't come home without her."

Humphrey struck an imploring pose with both arms curved towards his friend.

> "Father, forgive me. Shall I tell you true?
> Look on my shoulders, they are black and blue.
> Whilst to and fro fair Luce and I were winding,
> He came and basted me with a … a hedge-binding."

"Get men and horses," cried Venturewell. "We will be there within an hour. You will know the place again?"

Humphrey agreed, in his usual laborious verse.

> "I know the place where he my loins did swaddle.
> I'll get six horses, and to each a saddle!"

"Meanwhile," Venturewell concluded over the audience's combined groans and laughter, "I will go talk with Jasper's father."

The two men exited simultaneously though separately, one through the door on the left and the other through the door on the right.

"Georgie," said Nell, "what will you bet me now, that Master Humphrey will not finally have his Miss Luce? Tell me, Georgie, what will you wager?"

"You're a dreamer, Nell my sweet. That Jasper will be as far north as Puckeridge with her by now."

"Nay, Georgie, they are city folk walking in a wood, and besides it is dark, and I do not see how he could have gotten out of Waltham forest with her yet."

"Nay, cony, what will you bet me, that Rafe has not found her yet?"

"I will not wager against Rafe, honey, because I have not spoken with him. – But look, Georgie, peace! Here comes the merry old gentleman again."

Old Master Merrythought had returned to the stage, and wasted no time in bursting into song.

> *"When it was grown to dark midnight,*
> *And all were fast asleep,*
> *In came Margaret's grimly ghost,*
> *And stood at William's feet."*

The old fellow continued in prose, "I have money, and meat, and drink beforehand, till tomorrow at noon. Why-ever should I be sad? I feel as if I have half-a-dozen jovial spirits within me!

> *"I am three merry men, and three merry men!*

"To what end should any man be sad in this world? Give me a man who sings when he goes to his hanging, and a woman who will sing a catch in her travail! Never trust a tailor who does not sing at his work, for his mind is on nothing but filching."

"Oh my god, Georgie, that's so true. My tailor, you know, never sings, and he had four yards to make this gown, and I'll be sworn that Mrs Penistone, the draper's wife, had one made the same with only two."

Master Merrythought ignored this exchange, and struck up another song.

> *"'Tis mirth that fills the veins with blood,*
> *More than wine, or sleep, or food;*
> *Let each man keep his heart at ease*
> *No man dies of that disease.*
> *He that would his body keep*
> *From diseases, must not weep;*
> *But whoever laughs and sings,*
> *Never he his body brings*
> *Into fevers, gouts, or rheums,*
> *Or lingeringly his lungs consumes,*
> *Or meets with aching in the bone,*
> *Or catarrhs or griping stone;*
> *But contented lives for aye;*
> *The more he laughs, the more he may."*

"What do you say to this, Georgie? Is he not a fine old man? – God's blessing on thy sweet lips, Master Merrythought!" Nell laughed when Merrythought blew her kisses, before turning again to her wife. "When will you be so merry, Georgie? Lord, you are the frowningest little thing in the country when you are angry."

"Peace, cony," said Georgiana. "You shall see him taken down too, mark my words, and think of what he's about to hear. Here's the merchant, Luce's father, come now."

Merrythought, of course, greeted Venturewell with a snatch of song.

"As you came from Walsingham,
From that holy land,
There met you not with my true love
By the way as you came?"

"Oh, Master Merrythought," cried Venturewell, "my daughter's gone! This mirth becomes you not. My daughter's gone!"

"Why, if she be gone, what care I?
Let her come, or go, or tarry."

Venturewell was distraught. "Mock not my misery. It is your son Jasper – who I made my own, when all others forsook him – who has stolen my only joy, my child, away."

"He set her on a milk-white steed,
And himself upon a grey;
He never turned his face again,
But he bore her quite away."

"You are unworthy of the kindness I have shown to you

and yours! It is all too late, but now I see that you consent to my daughter's loss. Perhaps you were even complicit!"

"Your daughter!" Merrythought protested. "What a fuss you are making about your daughter! Let her go, think no more about her, but sing loud. I tell you, if both my sons were on the gallows, I would sing,

> *"Down, down, down they fall;*
> *Down, and arise they never shall."*

The poor suffering father cried, "Oh, might I behold her once again, and she once more embrace her agèd sire!"

Merrythought shrugged him off once more. "Fie, how scurvily this goes!

> *"She cares not for her daddy, nor*
> *She cares not for her mammy,*
> *For she is, she is, she is, she is*
> *My lord of Lowgave's lassy."*

By now Venturewell was made furious. "For this thy scorn I will pursue that son of thine to death."

"Do so, and when you have killed him,

> *"Give him flowers enough, pilgrim, give him flowers*
> *   enough;*
> *Give him red, and white, and blue, green, and yellow."*

"I'll fetch my daughter –"

"I'll hear no more about your daughter, sir, it spoils my mirth."

"I say, I'll fetch my daughter and –"

> *"Was never man for lady's sake,*
> *Down, down,*
> *Tormented as I, poor Sir Guy,*
> *De derry down,*
> *For Lucy's sake, that lady bright,*
> *Down, down,*
> *As ever men beheld with eye,*
> *De derry down."*

"– and I'll be revenged, by Heaven!"

Both fathers turned their backs and left the stage, each through different exits – Venturewell stalking in anger, and Merrythought bouncing along to his endless tune.

◆

Interlude 2

The musicians in the gallery began playing a tune to entertain the audience during the break. Nell and Georgiana got up, as if needing to stretch their legs.

"How do you like this, Georgie?" Nell asked.

"Why, I like it well, cony. But if Rafe would bestir himself, we would see more and better."

"The fiddlers go again, wife."

"Aye, Nell, but this is scurvy music. You were right: it would be much better with accordions. I wonder that they couldn't find any to play, for I gave the boy ample cash. – Hey, musicians!" Georgiana called. "Play 'Never Gonna Give You Up', won't you!"

"No, Georgie, let's have 'Silly Love Songs'!"

Georgiana gazed upon her wife fondly, and took her hand. "Why, surely this *is* a silly love song, cony. For they all are."

The couple dwelled together in a rare moment of peace … and then Sam advanced onto the stage with a new board on which was inscribed 'Privy Break'. He displayed it to the audience on either side, and to those in front of the stage. People began shifting and gathering their things – all the more so when two backstage staff dressed all in black came out to begin trimming the candles.

But it was only when Nell noticed the 'Privy Break' board and cried "Oh, thank the good Lord above!" that anyone dared move. She dashed out through the entrance to the Pit, with Georgiana not far behind her – and the audience followed when they could, chuckling all the way.

◆

Backstage

Dale had already dashed off for his own comfort break, and now he was on the hunt for Topher. He drew a blank in the dressing room and the green room, and in reception, so Dale tried outside, though Topher wasn't one of their few smokers and vapers. That's where he was, though; out in the service yard, staring up at the night sky in which a few stars bravely out-twinkled all of London's lights. It was cold, of course, so Topher had a big black overcoat slung on round his shoulders – and when he turned away with restless feet, Dale almost lost him in the shadows.

"*Topher*," Dale murmured as he came close, feeling the shape of the name made by the breath in his mouth. "*Topher.*"

"Oh god, is it time?" The startled Topher took a jerky step towards the stage door. "I lost track – How long – ?"

"No, no," Dale reassured him, presuming to settle a hand on his arm. "They're barely at the interval. You've got fifteen or twenty minutes yet."

"Oh, thank heavens for that." Topher heaved a sigh, and for a moment collapsed down to rest his hands on his knees, before straightening up again and re-grasping the coat across his chest.

"Are you okay?" Dale asked. "I didn't mean to give you a scare!"

"Yeah, yeah, I'm fine." Topher gave him a smile that seemed somewhat brittle despite himself, and then turned away a bit, to again gaze up at the night sky.

"So … Topher … I've been thinking."

"Uh oh," said Topher, looking at him again and betraying real apprehension for a moment.

"Old Master Merrythought," said Dale: "he'd be impossible in real life."

"Well, yeah."

"He's got a point, though."

Topher was mildly intrigued. "What's that, then?"

Dale had to take a breath before continuing, though this wasn't yet the hard bit. "Happiness is important."

Topher huffed a laugh, and his breath fogged in the cold air. "Thanks for the tip, Sherlock. Look," he added, "we'd better get in. Three acts to go, and we don't want to lose our voices."

"Wait a minute. Topher –" Dale found himself grinning, and utterly meaning it, too. There was that sense again of something unexpected surging up within him, as if it were air bubbling up from where it had long been trapped under deep dark water. "Topher, yes. Come home with me tonight. We'll celebrate, like we did last time." He tilted his head closer to confide, "It was good, you know, us celebrating."

"Oh, I know," Topher muttered under his breath. He was looking off to one side, as if considering something else entirely, or maybe just studiously avoiding Dale's gaze.

"Thought I should schedule some time for happiness, yeah?"

Topher finally looked at him directly. "Did you now … ?" This was delivered in tones too flat to actually signify a question. Topher let out a sigh. "So, that's tonight, then, is it? Tonight, and that's all."

"Yes," said Dale – and he let his voice soften into

fondness. "Like last time. Not such a bad tradition to follow."

A searching glance took in Dale's surprising vulnerability – he was as surprised as Topher at his own vulnerability in this moment – but Dale did not put his public mask back into place.

All Topher eventually said, though, was, "I'd better get in. Need to warm up my voice."

"Topher –"

"Come on," Topher said briskly, already two paces past him towards the door. "God, you didn't even put a coat on, you mad idiot."

"Topher, for god's sake …" Dale caught up with him, and muttered in the man's ear, conscious of the smokers and vapers loitering not so far away. "Is that a no?"

Topher cast him a sharp glance. "Yes, it's a no. We're both full of surprises tonight, aren't we?"

"But you're the one who asked me – before the show –"

"Well, I've had time to think, too." They had reached the stage door, which Topher opened before ushering Dale in. Once they were both inside and out of the cold, Dale assumed Topher would explain – but instead he only said, "I'm on next, all right? I need to warm up again." And off he jogged, up the stairs towards the green room.

Dale stood there for a stupidly dazed while, watching him go – long after Topher was actually out of sight – until finally he muttered to himself, "But then why did you kiss me, you great …" He'd been intending to go with 'pillock', but instead Dale sighed and concluded in defeated and oddly fond tones, "Ah, you great pudding."

◆

Act Three

The candles were trimmed and glowing brightly, and the audience had reassembled in good order. Sam had managed to hang up the 'Waltham Forest' sign on the tiring house façade without being accosted by the Citizens. The musicians were playing a tune that slowly wound its way into a sense of unease. And Jasper and Luce entered the stage.

"Come, my dear," said Jasper. "Though we have lost our way, we have not lost ourselves. Are you not weary with this night's wandering, and frightened by the darkness of this wild unpeopled place?"

"Neither," Luce gamely replied. "I cannot fear, or entertain a weary thought, while my best friend stands by me. You are the end of all my full desires, Jasper. Let those who lose their hopes, and live to languish as forsaken lovers, count the long steps and number time, start at a shadow, and shrink up their blood in fear – while I, quiet and content, take my pretty love in an embrace."

They gently hugged each other, and Jasper pressed an affectionate kiss to her brow before saying, "Come, sit down and rest." The two of them settled together on the ground. "Will you sleep, Luce?"

"I cannot sleep. Indeed, I cannot, friend."

"Why, then, we'll sing, and see if that might work upon our senses."

"I'll sing, or recite poetry, or do anything but sleep."

Jasper smiled. "Come, little mermaid; rob me of my

heart with that enchanting voice."

"You mock me, Jasper," she said with a happy laugh.

The two of them sang a love duet, which wasn't overly mawkish – not when it contained exchanges such as:

"Tell me more, are women true?"
"Some love change, and so do you."

But eventually Luce could stay awake no longer, and she curled up on the ground and surrendered to sleep.

Jasper watched over her for a few moments with peaceable fondness. "Sleep, sleep, and quiet rest crown thy sweet thoughts! Keep from her fair blood all horrors and fearful shapes! Let all her dreams be joys, and chaste delights, and such new pleasures as the transported soul gives to the senses!" He sighed with a poignant smile to see her slumber, and gently stroked her hair. "Keep her, you powers divine, while I contemplate the wealth and beauty of her mind!

"She is fair and kind and constant – and all this only to thee, Jasper. Oh, my joys!" He frowned, and turned away from the sight of his love. "Some say, however mockingly, that the sea and women are governed by the moon; both ebb and flow, both full of changes. Yet the wise know these opinions are but mischief: teasings and tauntings to bring on a pleasing war between men and women. It is said that the spiky fear of loss, and then the warmth of reassurance, are the most delicious parts of love. Who am I to say they're wrong?"

Jasper stood and paced away, running a despairing hand back through his hair. (Dale, watching from backstage, ached for that despair. He knew Topher hated this bit.) "I am being ridiculous. I have a love without the faults of women or men! And certainly I am certain of her love. But I shall test her, as a demonstration – and then the world shall sing her praises for ever after as the mirror of constancy."

He drew his dagger.

From the audience, Nell let out an ear-curdling scream, which made even Jasper and the slumbering Luce twitch.

Jasper quickly regathered himself, however, and cried, "Luce! Luce! Awake!"

The young woman woke from pleasant dreams, and was surprised to find Jasper standing there on restless feet with his dagger in his hand. "Why do you frighten me, friend, with those unhappy looks? Why are you drawn? Who has offended you?" She offered him a reassuring smile, and lifted her hand to invite him to join her. "I pray thee, Jasper, sleep. You've been watching the forest for danger for so long that you've turned wild."

"Come, make your way to Heaven," Jasper said harshly, "and bid the world with all its villainies farewell. You're for the next life, if there is one."

Luce was genuinely scared now. "Oh, Jasper! How can a young woman like myself have committed such evil to deserve this? Especially against the man I love!"

"Foolish girl," he rasped. "Can you imagine I could love the daughter of the man who flung me from my fortune into nothing? Discharged me from his service, shut the doors upon my poverty, and scorned my prayers, sending me, like a boat without a mast, to sink or swim? Come," he said, brandishing his fist wrapped round the dagger's hilt, "by this hand you die. I must have life and blood, to repay me for your father's wrongs."

In the front row, Nell was on her feet, both hands at her mouth, absolutely distraught. "Away, Georgiana, away! Find a policeman! Find a phone! Have them arrest this desperate villain! – Now, I charge you all," she cried to the audience members around her, "to see the Queen's peace kept! – Oh, my heart, what a scoundrel is this, to threaten murder to this harmless gentlewoman!"

Georgiana was sitting there fuming. "I promise you, sweetheart, we'll see justice done."

Even the good-humoured Verity was growing tired of all these interruptions to her performance. When she realised she could continue, she resumed her poignant pose, and Luce cried, "Oh, Jasper, be not cruel! If you will kill me, then smile, and do it quickly. Don't make me wait and imagine it a hundred times over. I am a woman, and right now I'm made of nothing but fear and love. Kill me not with your eyes; they shoot me through and through. Strike, Jasper, I am ready; and, dying, still I love you."

Venturewell and Humphrey made a timely entrance. "Whereabouts?" cried Luce's father.

"No more of this," Jasper muttered to himself. "I'll be true again."

"There, there he stands," said Humphrey, "with knife drawn in his hand, like a martial knight."

Venturewell demanded, "Sirrah, restore my daughter!"

"Sirrah, I will not," Jasper retorted.

"Upon him, then!"

In a clumsy show of brute force, Venturewell and Humphrey attacked Jasper – beating and cutting – and when he fell back a step or two, they dragged Luce away from him. Luce went willingly enough.

Nell, of course, was cheering them on. "That's it! Down with him, down with him, down with him! Cut him in the leg, boys, cut him in the leg!"

"Come with us, wretch," Venturewell said to Luce. "I'll provide a cage for you, seeing as a house wasn't strong enough."

Humphrey put his arm around Luce's waist to support her – and whether it was due to Jeremy's feelings for Verity, or Humphrey's for Luce, his quiet tenderness was an effective counterweight to her father's nastiness. "Truly," murmured Humphrey, "I'm glad our forces have the day."

The three of them exited the stage, leaving Jasper collapsed on the forest floor, alone and bleeding.

He twisted in pain for a moment, and then in agony. "They are gone, and I am hurt; my love is lost, never to get again. Unhappy Jasper, bleed and die!" He glared at his wounds for a moment, but they were not bad enough to oblige him. "Oh, my own folly has betrayed me! Hope has fled. I shall not see my love again; oh, no! She will not deign to look upon her butcher, and nor should she. Yet I must try."

Jasper staggered up to his feet, and swayed there for a moment. "Oh, Chance, or Fortune – or whatever you are that men adore as powerful – hear my cry. Let me loving live, or losing die!"

And he left the stage.

A tense silence filled the auditorium.

Nell had hidden her face in her hands during Jasper's

last speech. Finally she said, "Is he gone, Georgie?"

"Aye, cony."

"Good! Let him go, I pray you, sweetheart. By the faith of my body, he has put me into such a fright, that I tremble (as they say) like an aspen-leaf. Look at my little finger, Georgie, how it shakes. Now, in truth, every bit of me is doing the same."

Georgiana drew her down to the bench, to sit close beside her, and she wrapped Nell up in a warm embrace. "Come, sweet mouse; he shall not fright thee any more. Oh, my own dear heart, how you quiver!"

◆

Meanwhile, Dale had been waiting for Topher backstage – and when Topher saw him, they both broke into sheepish, reluctant smiles. Dale wasn't sure who had started it, but it was catching.

"That's another thing I won't miss," Topher whispered in Dale's ear, for fear of the sound carrying.

"You hate playing the villain," Dale agreed.

"That scene was always horrible. And I mean, this idea in all those old plays, that lovers should test each other – what were they even thinking?"

Dale averred, "If I could, I'd play all the villains for you –" *so you could always be the hero.*

Topher was staring at him, wide-eyed. He'd understood – or enough, at least, to guess the rest.

And it really had been such an incredibly stupid thought to offer, and melodramatic to boot. Dale shrivelled up inside, silently castigating himself –

And of course the others were ready to go on, and the Stage Manager was beckoning him urgently –

But Topher managed to squeeze his fingers reassuringly as Dale brushed past him, so it was perfectly easy to regain Rafe's good spirits as the Knight and his companions burst back onto the stage with tankards of beer in hand.

◆

"Oh, Rafe!" cried Nell, immediately brightening. "How are you, Rafe? Did you sleep well last night? Is that inn any good? How many stars would you give it?"

"Peace, Nell," said Georgiana. "Let Rafe alone."

The host and the tapster were waiting on Rafe at the Bell Inn, their solemn faces providing a clear contrast to the happy carousing of Mistress Merrythought, Michael, Rafe, Frank and Tim.

After a moment, the tapster muttered in the host's ear, "Master, they haven't yet paid the bill."

The merrily oblivious Rafe raised his tankard in a toast to the host. "Right courteous knight – who, for the order's sake, hangest out the holy Bell, as I this flaming Pestle bear about – we render thanks to your awesome self, your beauteous lady, and your gentle squires, for this refreshing of our wearied limbs, stiffened with hard adventures in the wild desert."

"Sir," said the tapster to Rafe, "there is twelve shillings to pay."

Rafe gurgled a laugh. "Oh, merry Squire Tapstero, thank you for comforting our souls with jugs of ale."

"Hurrah!" cried his companions, toasting the tapster and each downing another mouthful from their tankards.

"If fortune calls you forth, jovial squire," Rafe continued, "to follow the scent of adventure, then may you find just such kind hospitality from every true knight and every damsel fair."

The host now spoke. "Thou valiant Knight of the Burning Pestle, listen carefully. There is twelve shillings to pay, and no discounts no matter how prettily you declaim."

"Georgie, tell me," Nell asked in consternation, "must Rafe pay twelve shillings now?"

"No, Nell, no. The old fellow is jesting. Barkeeps were ever thus!"

"Oh, that's all right, then. Rafe can play along with a joke as well as anyone."

Rafe was suitably encouraged. "Sir Knight, this mirth of yours becomes you well. However, to repay your generous courtesy, if any of your squires wish it, he shall receive from my heroic hand a knighthood, by the virtue of this Pestle."

"Fair knight, this is a noble offer, but of no use to me. Therefore, twelve shillings you must pay, or I will have you arrested."

The tapster followed up the host's declaration by going to Rafe and taking a firm grasp of the neckline of his chainmail, before yanking him down into a stooped position.

Nell was on her feet at the edge of the stage. "Look, Georgie! Didn't I tell you? The knight of the Bell means every word. Give him his money, Georgie, and then he can go hang himself for all I care."

"Arrest Rafe!" Georgiana grumbled in protest as she got up and climbed the stairs to the stage. "Arrest Rafe, I ask you … All right, stop right there, Sir Knight of the Bell. Here's your money." She took out her wallet from her trouser pocket, and handed over a couple of ten-pound notes. "Have you anything to say to Rafe now? Arrest Rafe, indeed!"

"You should know," added Nell from the Pit, "that Rafe has friends who will not suffer him to be unjustly treated, even for ten times as much – and ten times more on top of that." As Georgiana returned to their seats, Nell gestured magnanimously. "You're free to continue, Rafe."

But Mistress Merrythought took the opportunity of the interruption to cease her adventures and return to her own play, *The London Merchant*. "Come, Michael, we'll go home to your father. He still has enough left to keep us for a day or two, and we'll send out fellows to search for our purse and our casket. Shall we go home, Michael?"

"Aye, mother, forsooth. In truth, my feet are full of chilblains with all this travelling."

Nell had been going to sit down, but now she turned back to offer her advice. "To be sure, those chilblains are a foul trouble. Mistress Merrythought, when your boy comes home, let him rub all the soles of his feet, and his heels, and his ankles with a mouse-skin. Or, if none of your people can catch a mouse, then try a potion of witch hazel, and I swear he shall be well."

Mistress Merrythought had been staring at Nell in horror through all this, but now she shook herself, and turned back to Rafe. "Master Knight of the Burning Pestle, my son Michael and I bid you farewell, and we thank you heartily for your kindness."

"Farewell, fair lady," Rafe replied, "and likewise to your tender squire. If while adventuring through these deserts, I do hear of any traitorous knight, who through his guile has lit upon your casket and your purse, I will despoil him of them, and restore them to you."

"I thank you, sir," she said, with a respectful curtsey. And then she and Michael left the stage.

Rafe stood tall, readying himself for his next adventure. "Dwarf, bear my shield. Squire, elevate my lance. And now I will bid you farewell, Knight of the holy Bell."

"Aye, Rafe," said Georgiana, "the bill is fully paid."

"But before I go, worthy knight," Rafe continued to the host, "tell me if you know of any quests a knight-errant might undertake, and through his prowess win eternal fame, and free some gentle souls from unjustified bonds or pain."

The host chuckled to himself, and beckoned the tapster close to speak to him confidentially. "Friend, go to Nick the barber, and tell him to prepare himself, as I told you before, quickly."

The tapster chuckled, too, and with a nod of agreement left the stage.

"Sir Knight," said the host to Rafe, "this wilderness affords none but The Great Venture, where many a knight has tried his prowess, and all ended in shame. I would not have you lose your life against a creature who is no man but a furious fiend of Hell."

"Speak on, Sir Knight," Rafe replied. "Tell me what he is and where. For here I vow, upon my blazing badge, never to waste a day in quietness, but only bread and water will I eat, and the green herb and rock shall be my couch, till I have quelled the man, or beast, or fiend who does such damage to knights-errant."

The host began to tell the tale of Barbarossa, the fearsome giant; the joke being that the host was really talking about Nick the barber-surgeon, but using 'high astounding terms' to concoct a chivalrous tale.

> "… in his hand
> He shakes a naked lance of purest steel,
> With sleeves turned up; and him before he wears
> A motley garment, to preserve his clothes
> From blood of those knights which he massacres …"

Rafe and his two companions were listening all agog.

> "… no sooner gentle knights can knock,
> But the shrill sound fierce Barbarossa hears,
> And rushing forth, brings in the errant knight,
> And sets him down in an enchanted chair;
> Then with an engine, which he hath prepared,
> With forty teeth, he claws his courtly crown …

> "Whilst with his fingers, and an instrument
> With which he snaps his hair off, he doth fill
> The wretch's ears with a most hideous noise:
> Thus every knight-adventurer he doth trim,
> And now no creature dares encounter him."

Rafe was hardly going to refuse such a challenge. "In God's name, I will fight with him. Kind sir, show me the way to this dismal cave, where this huge giant Barbarossa dwells.

"I doubt not that I'll curb this traitor foul,
And to the devil send his guilty soul."

(Rafe's fine confidence was lost towards the end of that speech, as he realised he wasn't going to be able to rhyme 'soul' with 'foul', no matter how he mangled things. It was a joke that Dale, as a child, had first seen played on *The Goodies* and had loved ever since.)

The host replied, "Brave-spirited knight, I'll bring you within sight of that most loathsome place, inhabited by an even more loathsome man – but I dare not stay longer."

"Saint George, set on before!" came Rafe's battle cry. "March, squire and page!"

And the host led the chivalric band off the stage and into an adventure.

◆

"Georgie," said Nell, "do you think Rafe will confound the giant?"

"I bet he will, Nell. Remember we watched him wrestle with the great Dutch strong-man at the fair, and hurl him to the ground?"

Nell gurgled with filthy laughter. "True, and that Dutchman was a goodly fellow, if all things were answerable to his bigness. But didn't you hear? There was a Scotchman taller than him, and the two of them met for a match to settle the difference, but it all came to nothing."

Mistress Merrythought appeared and took centre stage for her big scene, standing tall, and lifting and sweeping out her hands to strike a dramatic pose.

"Oh, look, Georgie," cried Nell, "here comes Mistress Merrythought again! But I want Rafe to come out and wrestle with the giant. I love a good fight scene! I tell you, I am hanging out to see it."

Georgiana stood, and gestured towards Mistress Merrythought to gain her attention.

Mistress Merrythought visibly sagged.

"My good woman," said Georgiana, "begone, I pray you, for my sake. Be patient a little while, and you shall have the audience then. I have some business to conduct."

It seemed that Mistress Merrythought might explode with frustration at this. She stood there with her fisted hands on her hips, glaring at the Citizens.

"Mistress Merrythought," Nell said, with an attempt at conciliatory tones, "if it please you to refrain your passion a little, till Rafe has despatched the giant out of the way, we shall think ourselves much obliged to you."

The woman turned and stalked off the stage, her shoulders sharp with fury.

"I thank you, good Mistress Merrythought," Nell called after her.

(That little scene was one of Dale's favourite bits of the whole play, and their Mistress Merrythought got every ounce possible out of it.)

Georgiana called, "Boy, come here!" When Sam entered, Georgiana demanded, "Send us out Rafe and this blasted giant, and make it quick."

"Truly, madam grocer, we cannot. You'll utterly spoil

our play, and have us hissed off the stage – and we'll still have to pay for the venue! Yet you will not let us go on with our plot." Sam pleaded to the audience, "I pray you, ladies and gentlemen, overrule her."

Georgiana would not be deterred. "Let Rafe come now and do this scene, and I'll trouble you no more."

Sam looked very sceptical at such a promise. "Will you shake hands on that?"

"Shake his hand, Georgie, do – and I'll kiss him to seal the deal. I am sure the boy is honest and honourable."

Sam and Georgiana shook hands, and Sam said, "I'll send Rafe to you presently."

He obviously hadn't taken Nell seriously though, for he was about to turn and walk off the stage when she beckoned him closer – and closer – and closer still. Sam was as wide-eyed and stunned as any deer before the headlights, but undeniably interested. Soon he was kneeling on the edge of the stage, and stuttering out, "But your wife –"

"Oh, Georgie don't mind," Nell stoutly replied, not even glancing around for confirmation.

And all the while Sam had been leaning forward – and Nell had his head firm between both hands now, and was kissing him on the mouth, and with plenty of tongue for all anyone else might tell.

Georgiana rolled her eyes a little, but sat back down as if happy enough not to interfere.

When Nell was finally done, she let Sam go and said, "I thank you, little youth." Sam managed to get himself to his feet and scarper through the centre doors.

"To be sure," Nell remarked, stepping back to her seat

with a swagger in her hips, "the child has a sweet breath, Georgie. But I think he is troubled with the nerves. He would tremble and shake in my hands! Lime blossom and mistletoe are the only things in the world for nerves."

"Yes, lamb."

◆

Nell got her fight scene.

Sam danced in to hang up a red-and-white striped barber's pole and a copper basin, and danced back out again to creepily discordant music.

Then the host led in Rafe through the door on the right – with Frank and Tim following in a fearful huddle – and he gestured towards the main door. "Courageous knight, yonder is his mansion – where the spear and copper basin are! But I dare not stay longer; he will appear."

The host turned tail and left.

Even Rafe had to take a few moments to stiffen his resolve. "Oh, faint not, heart! Susan, my lady dear – the cobbler's maid in Milk-street, for whose sake I take these arms – oh, let the thought of thee carry thy knight through all adventurous deed, and, in the honour of thy beauteous self, may I destroy this monster Barbarossa!"

Rafe looked about him, and Frank nodded encouragingly.

"Knock, squire," Rafe said to Tim, "upon the basin, till it break with the shrill strokes, or till the giant speaks."

Tim gathered himself, and went to rap his knuckles against the copper. The sound echoed ominously from backstage.

And then the barber entered.

The character was supposed to be a giant, of course, so they were doubling Jeremy in the role – who was already tall – and he was on stilts as well. To enter through the main doors, he made a show of grasping the upper doorframe in one hand, and ducking under it, before lifting up … and up … to his full height.

Rafe was only marginally daunted, though Tim was shaking, and Frank was quite content to hide himself behind Tim and peer around his knocking knees.

"Oh, Georgie," cried Nell, "the giant, the giant! – Now, Rafe, fight for your life!"

"What idiot is this," demanded the barber, "who dares so rudely knock at Barbarossa's cell, where no man comes but leaves his scalp behind?"

"I, you traitorous rogue, the Knight of the Burning Pestle, sent by fate to punish all the sad crimes you have committed against gentle ladies and errant knights. Prepare yourself to give a strict account of all your beastly villainies."

"Foolhardy knight," the giant cried, taking down his barber's pole to use as a weapon. "Prepare yourself, for dead soon shalt thou be."

"Saint George for me!" Rafe cried.

"Gargantua for me!"

The two met and skirmished in centre stage, both clumsy and ineffective, though the giant had the edge through sheer size. Rafe had already proved through the bout with Jasper that he was no fighter, and Jeremy was game but not exactly deft on his stilts. Tim and Frank managed little more than to confuse the matter.

Adding to the mayhem, the Citizens provided loud

commentary, encouragement and advice.

"Fake a blow, Rafe, fake a blow!" yelled Georgiana, sounding quite familiar with street fights. "The giant is open on the left!"

"Fend him off, fend him off!" called Nell. "That's it! – Oh, Rafe's almost down, Rafe's almost down!"

"Susan, inspire me!" Rafe cried. "Now, have up again."

"Up, up, up, up, up! Just so, Rafe! Now, down with him, down with him, Rafe!"

"Fetch him over the hip, boy!" added Georgiana.

Rafe was only of average height, so his head came to somewhere barely above the giant's waist. Teamwork was the only answer.

Frank whistled to get Tim's attention – and Tim went down onto one knee so that Frank could jump onto his bent leg, and from there climb up to sit on Tim's shoulders, before Tim stood again.

Another whistle – and Rafe carefully tossed up the Pestle –

– with which Frank cracked the giant over the head.

As the giant was falling in a spin, Frank threw the Pestle in an arc back down to Rafe, who finished off the giant with another great whack.

"There, boy!" cried Nell, as the giant collapsed to the floor. "Now, kill, kill, kill, kill, kill, Rafe!"

"No," said Georgiana. "Get what you can out of him first."

Rafe went to stand over the giant, with his sword hilt held high in both hands, its point over the giant's chest. "Presumptuous man! See to what desperate end thy treachery hath brought thee! The just gods never prosper those who do despise them."

"I crave for mercy, as thou art a knight, and scorn to spill the blood of those who beg."

"Thou showed no mercy, nor shalt thou have any. Prepare thyself, for thou shall surely die."

Nell was watching all this in an agony of suspense. "Why doesn't Rafe kill this giant and have done with it? Surely, if Rafe lets him go, he will do as much hurt as ever."

"Not so, mouse," said Georgiana in complacent tones, "if Rafe could convert the heathen."

"Aye, Georgie, if he could convert him – but a giant is not so easily converted as one of us ordinary people. There's a pretty tale of a witch, who had the devil's mark about her (God bless us!) and a giant for her son, who was called Lob. Did you ever hear it, Georgie?"

"Peace, Nell." Georgiana indicated the surrounding audience. "Cony, I can tell, it's perfectly clear that the ladies and gentlemen like Rafe. We must let him finish the scene."

"Aye, Georgie, I see it well enough. – Good ladies and gents, I thank you all heartily for gracing my man Rafe, and I promise you shall see him oftener."

A wounded cry sounded from the stage, drawing even Nell's attention.

"Mercy, great knight!" the giant pleaded. "I do recant my ill, and henceforth never gentle blood will spill."

"I give thee mercy," Rafe replied. "But you must swear upon my burning Pestle, to keep the promise you have freely given."

"I swear and kiss." The giant struggled to prop himself up on his arms, and stretched up further to kiss the

Golden Pestle that Rafe held out to him.

"Depart, then," said Rafe, perhaps a bit too loftily, "and amend thy ways."

The host and tapster came out to help carry off the felled giant, perhaps remorseful about setting up their friend the barber.

Rafe said, "Come, squire and dwarf, the sun grows towards his set, and we have many more adventures yet."

The three of them exited the stage with heads held high and a happy humour.

"Now Rafe has the swing of it," Georgiana declared in approbation. "I know he would have beaten all the men and women in the house, if they had been set on him. One giant was nothing at all!"

"Aye, Georgie, but it is well as it is. I am sure these good ladies and gentlemen know what it is to overthrow a giant." If anyone could manage to talk over themselves, it would be Nell in her excitement. Now she cried, "But, look, Georgie! Here comes Mistress Merrythought, and her son Michael. – *Now* you are welcome, Mistress Merrythought. Now that Rafe is done, you may go on."

This invitation was met with a look not overly gracious. "Michael, my boy," said Mistress Merrythought, turning away from the Citizens with a snapping swirl of her skirts.

"Aye, forsooth, mother."

"Be merry, Michael, we are at home now – where I am sure, if they will let us in, we will find everything a topsy-turvy mess."

A happy tune was struck up by the musicians, both in the gallery and in the tiring house behind the stage. Someone back there let out a joyous whoop.

"Listen to that!" Mistress Merrythought cried. "Nothing changes. If I get in among them, I'll play them such a lesson that they'll have no wish to come scraping and sawing here again. – Why, Master Merrythought! Husband! Charles Merrythought!"

From within the house they could hear Old Master Merrythought singing even more nonsensically than usual.

> *"If you will sing, and dance, and laugh,*
> *And holler, and laugh again,*
> *And then cry, 'There, boys, there!' why, then,*
> *One, two, three, and four,*
> *We shall be merry within this hour."*

"Why, Charles, do you not know your own natural wife? I say, open the door, let me in – and turn out those mangy companions. They have been hanging about you for far too long. You are a gentleman, Charles, and an old man now, and father of two children – and I myself (though I say it) by my mother's side am niece to a worshipful gentleman."

Old Merrythought appeared in the musicians' gallery, to serenade his wife.

> *"Go from my window, love, go.*
> *Go from my window, my dear!*
> *The wind and the rain*
> *Will drive you back again;*
> *You cannot be lodged here.*

"Hark you, Mistress Merrythought," he declared. "You

who go upon adventures, and forsake your husband, because he sings with never a penny in his purse. Shall I think myself the worse? Faith, no, I'll be merry. You cannot come here. In this house there are none but lads of fine spirit. They have lived for a hundred years or more, but they look like they're still boys, for care never drank their blood dry, and want never made them warble,

"Heigh-ho, my heart is heavy."

The musicians had accompanied that line with funereal gloom, but now began another sprightly tune. Young Michael's feet began tapping in time, despite his mother's disapproving glare. The old man turned away and danced back inside.

"Why, Master Merrythought," his wife called after him. "What am I, that you should laugh me to scorn so abruptly? Am I not your fellow-feeler in all our miseries? Your comforter in health and sickness? Have I not brought you children?" She gestured towards Michael, who was well into the rhythm of the music by now. "And are they not like you, Charles? Look upon your own image, you hard-hearted man! And yet for all this –"

From inside came the hard-hearted man's reply:

"Begone, begone, my juggy, my puggy,
Begone, my love, my dear!
The weather is warm,
'Twill do thee no harm:
You cannot be lodged here.

"Be merry, boys!" Master Merrythought called to his companions. "Some light music, and more wine!"

Mistress Merrythought was left outside, thwarted, and looking about her as if wondering how to proceed. Michael was skipping around to the music, as if he didn't care where they'd lay their heads that night. But he was young, and could afford to be carefree. His mother could not.

Nell said, "That old man is not in earnest, I hope, Georgie – is he?"

"What if he is, sweetheart?" Georgiana softly replied.

"If he is, Georgie, I'll make bold to tell him he's an ignorant old man to use his bed-fellow so badly."

"What! How does he use her, honey?"

Nell stood, and took a couple of steps – and swept back around to scold her wife. "Don't you get saucy with me, Georgiana! I should have known you'd take his part in this."

Georgiana lifted her hand in elegant supplication. "Nell, don't chide me; for, as I am an honest woman and a true grocer, I do not like his doings."

"Then I forgive you, Georgie love," said Nell, taking her wife's hand in both her own. "You know we are all frail and full of infirmities." Nell turned to call loud enough to be heard in the tiring house: "D'you hear me, Master Merrythought? Might I crave a word with you?"

The old man appeared again in the gallery, though all he did was say to the musicians, "Strike up lively, lads!"

Nell, however, was not going to wait to be acknowledged, but let go of Georgiana and launched into her tirade. "I had not thought, in truth, Master

Merrythought, that a man of your age and discretion, as I may say, being a gentleman, and therefore known by your gentle attributes, could have shown so little respect to the vulnerabilities of his wife. For your wife is your own flesh, the staff of your age, your yoke-fellow, with whose help you draw through the mire of this transitionary world. Nay, she's your own rib, and again –"

Master Merrythought broke into resounding song, perhaps in direct response to Nell or perhaps not.

"I came not hither for thee to teach,
I have no pulpit for thee to preach,
I would you had kissed me under the breech,
As thou art a lady gay."

"Strike me down with a vengeance!" hollered Nell, while a pleased Mistress Merrythought looked on. "I am heartily sorry for the poor gentlewoman, but if I were your wife, greybeard, I'd –"

Georgiana got up at last, and offered soothing hands. "I ask you, sweet honeysuckle, be content."

"Using such words to me, who is as much a Citizen as any of them! Hang the hoary rascal!" Nell took a breath, and then another, and then said a little more quietly, "Get me a drink, Georgie. I am almost molten with fretting. Damn his knave's heart for it!"

Georgiana considered her fondly, dropped a gentle kiss to Nell's forehead; but then left through the Pit to go fetch drinks.

"Play me a light lavolta!" Master Merrythought said to the musicians. "Come, let's frolic. Top up every fellow's wine."

His wife called up, "Are you really going to make me wait out here? You'll open up the house, I trust – or I'll fetch those who'll open it for me."

"Good woman," he replied, "if you will sing, I'll give you something. If not –

> *"You are no love for me, Margaret,*
> *I am no love for you.*

"Come aloft, boys, aloft!" And he turned away again with an air of finality.

"Damn you, sir!" hollered Mistress Merrythought. "Come, Michael," she continued a little more reasonably, "we'll not trouble him further. We shall not be dependent on his whims! Come, boy, I'll provide for you, I promise faithfully. We'll go to Master Venturewell's, the merchant, and I'll ask him for a letter of recommendation to the host of the Bell in Waltham. There I'll place you as a prentice with the tapster. Will not that do well for you, Michael?"

The boy didn't seem too unenthusiastic at the idea of them making their own way in the world.

"Leave me to deal with that old knave, your father. I know how to treat him as we've been treated, I assure you!"

And the two left the stage together to go look for a new future.

◆

Backstage

Dale had tucked himself away in their corner of the dressing room, where anyone else would have respected his privacy, but it would have been entirely unreasonable of him to be surprised when Topher tracked him down.

Topher sat in his own chair, and swung around so he could meet Dale's gaze via the medium of Dale's mirror. They stared at each other for long moments, knowing there was no point in exchanging pleasantries or banalities.

Finally Topher said, "Look –"

When the pause went a fraction too long, Dale found himself prompting, "Yes?"

"Look," Topher continued, "the next time I go home with you – I promised myself – I won't be leaving in the morning."

Dale stared at him mutely, no doubt looking as if he felt under siege.

Topher sighed in sharp frustration. "You know what I mean. I'm not staging a sit-in. There's practicalities, and I'm not saying I should move in right away, or you with me. But the next time – I won't be leaving *you*. We're going to give it a try. Being together. For good."

"Not for evil?" Dale asked, aiming at a joke.

Topher ignored him, and steadily continued on. "I know a relationship doesn't fit into your Life Plan, or not for ages yet. But some things won't ever happen according to a schedule. Will they?" Another of his flat, rhetorical questions. "I mean, how can you plan for – ?"

"I know you, Topher," Dale came back directly. "You like the whole friends-with-benefits thing, I know you do."

"And no one could be more surprised than myself, but I guess sometimes you meet someone who makes you realise that's fine when it's fine, but it's not the whole story. Sometimes there's more happiness to be found in … in trying for more."

Dale took a long moment with this. Eventually he admitted, "It's oddly reassuring, how completely unromantic you're being."

"That's a good sign?"

"Maybe."

"Yeah, like maybe this could work."

"Maybe it could," Dale coolly agreed. "But not yet. Not yet, Toph. Like you said, it doesn't fit into the plan. And by the time I'm ready, you'll have moved on." He shrugged. "Our timing's off, that's all."

Topher's stare had turned into more of a glare. "Fuck's sake," he grumbled, standing up and turning away. "You really are being a complete idiot about this, Dale."

"You won't mind for too long, then, will you?" he pointed out in cheerful tones.

Topher growled in disgruntlement as he walked away.

◆

Interlude 3

There was movement at the doors behind the Pit, prompting Nell to call out, "Hurry up, Georgie, where's the beer?"

"Here, love," Georgiana replied. She had brought two plastic tumblers of the no-alcohol beer, and now handed one to Nell before taking her seat beside her wife.

Inevitably, Nell had another grumble about Old Master Merrythought: "This wicked old fellow will not get out of my mind."

Then Nell lifted her beer to the audience members around her. "Ladies and gents, I toast you all, and I desire more of your acquaintance with all my heart."

Sam entered the stage, and started dancing to a jig.

"Look, Georgie, that nice young man has come out again. Doesn't he look a bit like Prince William? Though with a bit more hair. I'll bet Prince William cannot caper about so sprightly as that, mind. Look at how he points his toe so elegant like! – Do a cartwheel, boy! Go on! Or flip yourself upside-down and walk on your hands!"

Sam did not oblige.

"Can you not do a cartwheel?"

"No," answered Sam, rather crestfallen.

"Can you juggle? Or eat fire?"

"Neither."

"Well, then, never mind," said Nell compassionately. "I thank you kindly for the jig." She dug in her purse for some change, and held it out to him. "There's two pounds to buy you something sweet."

Sam exited again, looking somewhat forlorn.

◆

Act Four

Jasper entered the stage, along with a boy carrying a leather satchel and wearing a cloth cap adorned with a small wing that signified Mercury, god of messages. Jasper handed the boy a sealed letter. "There, deliver this; do not fail me. And have you organised four strong fellows who are able to carry me? Is everything as I asked for?"

"Sir, you need not fear. The men are ready for you, and everything else is arranged."

"There, my boy," said Jasper, handing him a couple of small coins. "Don't spend it all at once!"

"In faith, sir, I'll try to control myself."

Jasper chuckled under his breath. "There'll be more for you when we're done."

The boy readied himself to depart. "I fly, and on my wings carry your destiny."

"Go, and be happy!" Jasper saluted the boy as he ran off stage, and then lifted his hands to the Heavens. "Now, my hope, forsake me not, but fling thy anchor out, and let it hold until my love enjoys my love once more!"

He left the stage in a fine state of high emotion …

… but Nell was unimpressed. "Yes, be off with you! You are as crooked a sprig as ever grew in London. – He'll come to some bad end or other, I'll bet anything you like, for his looks say no less. Besides, his father (you know, Georgie) is none of the best. You heard him disrespect me with his bawdy songs! In faith, if I live, Georgie –"

"Let me be, sweetheart," Georgiana replied. "I have a

trick in my head that shall land him in a world of trouble, and make him sing *peccavi* before I'm done – and yet he shall never know who hurt him neither."

"Do so, my good Georgie, do!"

Sam appeared on the stage, and Georgiana immediately demanded, "What shall we have Rafe do now, boy?"

"You shall have what you will, madam grocer."

"Why, then, sir, go and fetch me Rafe, and let the Shah of Persia come and christen the child Rafe got upon the Shah's beautiful niece."

Sam snorted. "Believe me, madam grocer, that will not do so well. It is a stale story and has been done before at the Red Bull. I think we can manage something a little better than what they do at the Red Bull, madam."

Nell chipped in. "Georgie, let Rafe travel over great hills, and let him be very weary, and come to the King of Cracovia's house, covered with black velvet – and there let the king's daughter stand in her window, all dressed in beaten gold, combing her golden locks with a comb of ivory – and let her spy Rafe, and fall in love with him, and come down to him, and carry him into her father's house – and then let Rafe … *converse* with her."

"Well done, Nell," Georgiana said bracingly. "It shall be so. – Boy, let's have it done, and quickly now."

Sam rolled his eyes and raised his hands in exasperation. "Madam, if you will imagine all this to be done already, you shall hear them talk together – but we cannot present a house covered with black velvet, and a lady dressed in beaten gold."

"Can you not?" Georgiana retorted. "I wonder if the Red Bull could do so. But never mind, let's have it as best you can, then."

"Anyway," Sam continued, "you can't have a grocer's prentice court a king's daughter. That's ridiculous! No one is going to suspend their disbelief that far."

"Is that so, sir?" Georgiana replied with icy sarcasm. "You are well read in histories! I ask you, what was Sir Dagonet before he came to King Arthur's court? Was he not apprentice to a grocer in London? Or if you read the play of *The Four Prentices of London*, where Eustace tosses his pike in a competition – you'll find that he, too, was a grocer's apprentice. I pray you, fetch Rafe in, sir, fetch Rafe in."

Sam had given up. "Then it shall be done." He backed away, and addressed the audience before slipping through the central doors: "Ladies and gentlemen, you see how it is. Please remember – none of this is our fault."

Nell declared, "Now we shall see fine doings, Georgie, for sure!"

Sam popped out again, writing in chalk on a board, which he then hung at the back of the stage: 'The King of Moldavia's Court'. He offered a distracted bow to the audience, then disappeared again.

Rafe then entered, with his squire and dwarf following along behind him in solemn procession. They took a turn about the stage and then stood to look up at the musicians' gallery in an expectant hush.

A long moment later, Pompiona appeared in the gallery – suddenly popping in, as if given a shove from backstage – and made her way to the balustrade. There she struck an overly elegant pose, showing off her golden gown. It seemed not to be fully fastened, as if she'd shrugged it on in unseemly haste, and her headdress of peacock feathers was askew. She was bearing a lantern containing lit candles, from which wafted an exotic spicy scent.

"Oh, here they are!" cried Nell. "Oh, how prettily the King of Cracovia's daughter is dressed!"

"Aye, Nell," said Georgiana in pedantic tones. "It is the fashion of that country, you know."

"But! But! But!" Nell was out of her seat again, and straining to see from the foot of the stage. "That's no lady! That's the guy from *EastEnders* again! You remember, Georgie? He plays that lovely Humphrey, and I swear he was the giant, too, now I think about it. And here he is again, as the princess!"

"Peace, cony," said Georgiana.

Offended by Nell yet again, Jeremy had drawn up to his full masculine height. He sniffed in disapproval – and then fell into a comic routine in which he let go of his golden dress to set his headdress aright, swapped the (supposedly) hot lantern to his other hand, then grabbed at his loose dress before it slipped down past his bare shoulders to reveal more than it should, reached to reset his headdress again when the peacock feathers fell forward over his face, swapped the lantern back, grabbed for his dress to hold it up, and round and round again …

Eventually, one of the musicians took pity on him, and came over to stand by his shoulder, holding up the lantern, as if she were Pompiona's attendant.

Jeremy was finally able to take on a more feminine shape again, and Pompiona gestured graciously to Rafe below. "Welcome, Sir Knight, unto my father's court,

King of Moldavia, and unto me, Pompiona, his daughter dear! But I fear we have offended you, if you will only stay with us for one night."

"Damsel right fair," said Rafe, "I am on many sad adventures bound, that call me forth into the wilderness. Besides, my horse's back is rather chafed, and I must ride at a sober pace. But many thanks, fair lady, be to you for dealing so courteously with an errant knight."

"But wait, brave knight! What is your name and birth?"

"My name is Rafe. I am an Englishman – as true as steel, a hearty Englishman – and prentice to a grocer in the Strand. But fortune called me to follow arms, and I took on the order of the Burning Pestle, which I bear before all men and confound the enemies of all ladies."

Pompiona was impressed, and eagerly yet gracefully leaned forward, the better to converse with Rafe. "Often have I heard of your brave countrymen, and of your fertile soil and store of wholesome food. My father sings the praises of a drink in England found, and Pale Ale called, which drives all the sorrow from your hearts."

"Lady, it's true," Rafe fervently replied. "There is nothing better to quench your thirst and lift your mind."

"And of Salted Beef and Mustard he will speak, in tones of reverence."

"Aye, lady."

Pompiona drew herself up again, and continued in a more dignified manner. "For there have been great wars betwixt us and you – but truly, Rafe, it was never my wish that it be so. Tell me then, Rafe, could you be happy and proud to wear this lady's favour in your shield?" Pompiona looked about her person for a suitable favour, but could find nothing more than a ribbon from her dress. She drew it out – which of course only loosened the dress further, so she had to clutch the golden fabric to herself with both hands to preserve her modesty.

Rafe replied with a noble face that did not deign to notice such teasing delights. "I am a knight of a religious order, and will not wear the favour of a lady who trusts in Antichrist and false traditions."

"Well said, Rafe!" called Georgiana. "Convert her, if you can."

"Besides," Rafe continued in less lofty tones, "I have a lady of my own in merry England, for whose virtuous sake I took these arms. Susan is her name, a cobbler's maid in Milk Street, whom I vow ne'er to forsake while Life and Pestle last."

"Happy is that lady Susan, who for her own, dear Rafe, has won you! Unhappy am I, who ne'er shall see again the man who bears my heart away!"

"Lady, farewell! I needs must take my leave."

"Hard-hearted Rafe, who can desert a lady so!"

"Rafe!" cried Georgiana, beckoning him over to the edge of the stage. "Rafe! Here's some money for you." She handed up a number of coins from her wallet. "Distribute it generously in the King of Cracovia's house. Be not beholding to him."

Rafe took it with his usual earnest seriousness, and returned to address Pompiona. "Lady, before I go, I must remember your father's officers, who have been so very diligent. Hold out thy snowy hand, thou princely maid! There's twelve-pence for your father's chamberlain –"

Pompiona leaned over the balustrade, still clutching her

clothes together with one hand, and stretching the other down towards Rafe, while every now and then having to reach up to prevent her peacock feathers from falling into her face. Of course, no matter how far Rafe stretched up on tiptoe, they couldn't quite reach each other. So Frank the dwarf climbed up Tim the squire again – and this time stood on his shoulders. Rafe gave the coin to Tim, who handed it up to Frank, who then passed it on to Pompiona.

"And another shilling for his cook," Rafe continued, handing over the coin, "for the goose was roasted full well. And twelve-pence for your father's horse-keeper, for anointing my horse's poor back. To the maid who washed my boot-hose there's an English groat –"

Of course, there was a time lag between Rafe's declarations and the coins actually being placed in Pompiona's hand, so she was getting rather confused, trying to keep the amounts and recipients aligned. Added to which, her headdress was coming loose, and she didn't have a spare hand to set it right.

"– and tuppence to the boy who wiped my boots. And last, fair lady, there is for yourself thruppence, to buy you hairpins at the market."

"Full many thanks," said Pompiona, looking rather relieved that it was all over.

"Advance, my squire and dwarf! I cannot stay."

"You slay my heart in leaving me this way."

The grief-stricken Pompiona took the lantern from the musician and withdrew into her father's palace in a flustered hurry, while Rafe led his brave and resourceful companions off-stage.

"I commend Rafe," Nell announced, "for not being seduced by a Cracovian, even if she is a princess. There are women aplenty in London longing for his return."

"Aye, cony," Georgiana agreed, giving her wife a wry look.

Venturewell now entered the stage through the main doors, with Luce behind him. They were pacing slowly and deliberately, seeming serious and a bit self-conscious – and when a young servant in an apron followed them, he kept glancing back as if they were waiting on someone.

Sure enough, a moment later, Humphrey stumbled in after Jeremy had hastily discarded Pompiona's golden gown. He was clutching Humphrey's hat in one hand – though he was safely oblivious to a peacock feather that remained stuck in his hair. Humphrey drew himself up into his familiar self-importance.

Nell cried, "Here is Master Humphrey and his love again, Georgie!"

"Aye, cony; peace."

Venturewell addressed his daughter in some fury. "Go, get you to your chamber; I will not be entreated. And I'll keep you safe hereafter from gadding about with reckless youths. Do not try to move me with your tears! I know too well you can turn your weeping on and off at will."

"Father," said an honestly distressed Luce, "you do me wrong – but I confess that Jasper has done me a worse wrong."

"Go, sirrah," Venturewell said to the servant, handing him a bundle of keys. "Lock her in, and keep the key safe as you love your life."

Luce and the boy left the stage in silence.

"Now, my son Humphrey," said Venturewell, "you may rest assured of my continued love, and prepare to reap your desire."

"I see this love you speak of," Humphrey solemnly replied, "and will return it in every way I can, as befits a Christian and a gentleman."

"And so my daughter is yours again. Appoint the time, and take her – but I pray you, no more games. I myself and some few of our friends will see you married."

"I would that *you* would name the day!" Humphrey shuddered, which set the peacock feather to shimmering in the candlelight (and Venturewell had to make a visible effort to ignore it). "And make it soon, for I ever was afraid to lie alone."

"Some three days hence, then."

Humphrey took a moment to consider this proposal, and then huffed out a long breath. "Three days! Let me see. It is somewhat longer than I'd hoped – yet I agree, for it gives me time to visit all my friends in new array."

The serving boy entered again, to announce, "Sir, there's a gentlewoman without who would speak with your worship."

"Who is she?"

"Sir, I asked her not."

"Well, bid her come in."

The servant left, and Mistress Merrythought and Michael entered.

"Peace be to your worship!" she said. "I come as a poor suitor to you, sir, in the behalf of this child."

Venturewell was eyeing her narrowly. "Are you not wife to Merrythought?"

"Yes, truly," she replied, oblivious to Venturewell's stony manner but not to Humphrey's nodding peacock feather, which she tried not to let distract her. "But would I had never seen Master Charles Merrythought! He has undone me and himself and his children; and there he lives at home, and sings and frolics and revels among his drunken companions! But, I warrant you, he does not know where to get a penny to put bread in his mouth – and therefore, if your worship will oblige me, I would entreat a letter from you to the honest host of the Bell in Waltham, that I may place my child under the protection of his tapster, in some settled course of life."

Now Venturewell let loose such a fierce scowl that Mistress Merrythought and Michael quailed before it. "The Heavens have heard my prayers! Thy husband, when I was ripe in sorrows, laughed at me. Thy son Jasper, like the most unthankful wretch to me who made him mine, to show his love again, first stole my daughter, then wronged this gentleman, and caused me grief that would have brought me down unto my grave, had not God's strength relieved my sorrows." He advanced on her and her son, looming large. "Go, and weep as I did, and be unpitied; for I here declare an everlasting hate to all who bear thy name."

Mistress Merrythought gathered herself, unnerved but determined. "Will you say so, sir? May God now teach you charity for those who are as beset by troubles as you yourself are. – Come, Michael, let this fine gentleman keep his wind to cool his porridge. We'll go to your nurse's, Michael. She knits silk stockings, and we'll knit too, boy, and be beholden to no one."

And with more dignity than she'd ever yet achieved, Mistress Merrythought left the stage with Michael beside her.

Now the messenger boy entered, bearing the letter from Jasper.

"Sir," he said to Venturewell, "I take it you are the master of this house."

"What of it, boy?"

"Then to yourself, sir, comes this letter." He handed it over with a flourish.

"From whom does it come, my boy?"

The messenger unconsciously shifted to a more heroic stance as he began to deliver his speech. "From him who was once your servant. But no more shall that name ever be, for he is dead. Grief over the anger he caused you broke his heart. I saw him die, sir, and from his hand received this paper, with a charge to bring it here. Read it, and satisfy yourself in all the details of his sad story."

Venturewell took the letter, unfolded it, and read it out loud. "*Sir, that I have wronged your love for me I must confess; and I have earned for myself, besides my own undoing, the ill opinion of my friends. Let not your anger, good sir, outlive me, but suffer me to rest in peace with your forgiveness. Let my body (if a dying man may so prevail upon you) be brought to your daughter, that she may truly know my flames are now quenched, and receive a testimony of the zeal I bore her virtue. Farewell for ever, and be ever happy! Jasper.*" Venturewell groaned, and crushed the letter to his heart. "God's hand is great in this! Poor, wretched Jasper. I do forgive him. Yet I am glad he's quiet, where I hope he will not bite again. –

Boy, bring the body, and let him have his will, if that be all."

"It is here without, sir."

"So, sir," replied Venturewell, "if you please you may conduct it in. I do not fear it."

Humphrey added, "I'll act as usher, boy; for he owed me something once, and well did pay it."

The two men followed the boy off the stage, with their heads respectfully bowed.

◆

The stage direction read: 'Enter Luce, alone.' Dale had to admit it gave his heart a wrench to see Verity pace onto the stage and then stand very still, with her upright bearing undercut by unhappiness.

After a quiet moment she moaned, and said, "If there be any punishment inflicted upon the miserable, more than yet I feel, let it altogether seize me, and at once press down my soul! I cannot bear the pain of these delaying tortures." She suddenly swirled in place, and bent as if broken, and lifted her hands in a simple plea. "Thou that art the end of all, and the sweet rest of all, come, come, oh, Death! Bring me to thy peace, and blot out all the memories I nourish of my father and of my cruel friend!"

The serving boy entered, under orders but wary of disturbing her further. He was carrying a table, which he placed in the centre of the stage. "By your leave, young mistress; here is a boy who has brought a coffin. I don't know what this is about, but your father charged me to give you notice. Here they come."

The messenger boy now led in four men bearing a simple coffin. It had no lid, but the body lying within it was covered with a black cloth. They placed it carefully on the table.

Luce said, "For me I hope this coffin is come, and it is most welcome!"

"Fair mistress," said the messenger, "let me not add greater grief to that great store you have already. Jasper (who while he lived was yours, now dead and here enclosed) commanded me to bring his body hither, and to crave a tear from those fair eyes to deck his funeral (though he knew he deserved not pity). For so he bid me tell her for whom he died."

Luce was stunned. She had been miserable before, but now something within her was crushed. It was the death of a Hope that she hadn't known she still cherished.

"Of tears," said Luce, "he shall have many." She heaved in a breath, a sob, before addressing her companions. "Good friends, depart a little, while I take my leave of this man who once I loved."

The men and boys left the stage.

Once she was alone again, Luce paced pensively around the coffin, before standing with a hand resting gently on one side. "Hold yet a little, life! And then I'll give thee to thy first heavenly being.

"Oh, my friend! You have got before me, but I shall not long be after. You were too cruel to yourself, Jasper, in punishing the fault I have already forgiven. You did not wrong me, but were ever most kind, most true, most loving. Did you ask for one tear only? I'll give you all my tears, all that my eyes can pour down, all my sighs, and all myself. Before you leave, there are a few small rites for me to perform; but if your soul is yet about this place, and can see what I prepare to bless you with, it shall go up, borne on the wings of peace, and satisfied.

"First will I sing your dirge, then kiss your pale lips, and then die myself, and fill one coffin and one grave together.

> *"Come, you whose loves are dead,*
> *And, whiles I sing,*
> *Weep, and wring*
> *Every hand, and every head*
> *Bind with cypress and sad yew;*
> *Ribbons black and candles blue*
> *For him that was of men most true!*
>
> *"Come with heavy moaning,*
> *And on his grave*
> *Let him have*
> *Sacrifice of sighs and groaning;*
> *Let him have fair flowers enough,*
> *White and purple, green and yellow,*
> *For him that was of men most true!"*

Luce slowly but resolutely shifted her hand across to grasp a fistful of the black cloth. "Sad cover of my joys, I lift thee up, and thus I meet with death." She tugged the cloth aside –

– and Jasper leapt up within the coffin! "And thus you meet the living," he cried.

Luce screamed and backed away, gathering up her

skirts so she could run. "Save me, Heaven!"

"No, do not fear me, fair one," Jasper reassured her, jumping down to the floor on the opposite side of the coffin. "I am no spirit. Look closer at me; do you know me yet?"

Staring hard at Jasper, Luce dared to approach nearer, and they finally met at the foot of the coffin. "Oh, you are the dear shadow of my friend!"

Jasper laughed a little, and took her hands in his. "Dear substance, I swear I am no shadow. Feel my hand; it is the same it was. I am your Jasper; your Jasper who is yet living, and yet loving."

They were standing so trustingly close by now, with their hands raised between them as if in a mutual prayer.

"Pardon my rash attempt," Jasper continued, "my foolish challenge of your constancy. Sooner should my dagger have drunk my own blood, and set my soul at liberty, than drawn the least drop from your body. For my idiocy, doom me to anything you wish. If you wish me death, I will take it, and willingly."

"This death I'll give you for it," she replied, and pressed a kiss to his mouth. They shared a smile of happy relief. "So, now that I am satisfied you are no spirit, but my own truest, truest, truest friend, answer me this: Why do you come to me in a coffin?"

"First, to see you; and then to convey you hence."

Luce shook her head. "It cannot be, for I am locked up here, and watched at all hours. It is impossible for me to escape."

"There is nothing more possible. Oh, I have the wits of twenty men about me! Creep into the coffin, love, and they will convey you hence. Fear nothing, dearest love. I must needs stay here for a little while, but I will make sure you are safe."

"Then I will indeed fear nothing, my friend. But come to me soon."

Jasper helped Luce get into the coffin, and once she was settled then he covered her with the black cloth. "Lie still, just so. All goes well yet." Jasper took a step away. "Boy!"

The messenger boy entered again, with the four men following him. "At hand, sir."

"Bear away the coffin, and be wary. That is the most precious burden of all you carry."

"It will be done as you wish, sir."

The men raised the coffin and carried it carefully off stage.

Jasper watched them go through the main doors, and then headed towards the side door on the right. "Now must I go conjure!"

◆

Venturewell entered again, and called for the messenger boy.

"Your servant, sir," said the boy as he returned to the stage.

"Do me this kindness, boy – Wait, here's five shillings for you. Before you bury the body of this fellow, carry the coffin to his old merry father, and salute him from me – and bid him sing, for he has cause."

"I will, sir."

"And then bring me word of what tune he is in – and have another five shillings – but do it truly. The old man deserves to be vexed."

With no sense of irony, the boy said, "God bless your worship's health, sir!"

"Farewell, boy!"

Venturewell and the boy each left the stage, while Merrythought entered through the door on the right in his usual cheerful mood.

"Old Merrythought!" called Nell. "Have you come again? Let's hear some of your songs."

"Aye," said Georgiana. "Sing now, old man, for you will have a shock soon enough."

Merrythought ignored the spoiler, but obligingly broke into song.

"Who can sing a merrier note
Than he that cannot change a groat?

"Not a ha'penny left, and yet my heart leaps. I do wonder yet, as old as I am, why any man will follow a trade or serve, who might instead sing and laugh and walk the streets. My wife and both my sons are I know not where; I have nothing left, nor do I know how I'll find meat for my supper; yet I am merry still, for I know I shall find my meal upon the table at six o'clock. Therefore, hang thought!

"I would not be a serving-man
To carry the cloak-bag still,
Nor would I be a falconer

"It is this that keeps life and soul together: mirth. This is the philosopher's stone that they write so much about, that keeps a man ever young."

A serving boy entered, and addressed him anxiously. "Sir, they say they know all your money is gone and you cannot pay, so they will not send you any more drink."

"Will they not?" cried Merrythought, still in good cheer. "Let them choose as they will! The best thing is that I have mirth at home, and need not send abroad for that. Let them keep their drink to themselves.

The boy was smiling fondly at the old man, his anxiety erased – but then another serving boy entered the stage. "Sir, I can get no bread for supper."

"Hang bread and supper!" cried Merrythought. "Let's preserve our mirth, and we shall never feel hunger, I'll warrant you. Let's have a catch, boys; follow me, come."

Merrythought led the way, and each of the others chimed in as his turn came, as they all three sang this round together:

> *"Ho, ho, nobody at home!*
> *Meat, nor drink, nor money have we none.*
> *Fill the pot, Edie,*
> *Never more need I."*

Merrythought finished with a hurrah. "So, boys, follow me. Let's change our place, and then we shall laugh afresh."

And they all danced off the stage while the musicians played a sprightly tune.

◆

Backstage

For some inexplicable reason, Dale found himself seeking out Topher – when actually it was Topher who was bursting at the seams to speak with Dale. Who knew why these things happened? Dale feared it was all beyond him to explain at this point. He and Topher ran into each other in an anonymous corridor.

"*That's* what it's about," Topher blurted out, grasping Dale's upper arms for emphasis. "*That's* what the play is about. Beaumont wrote it out as plain as day, and Merrythought just spoke it."

"What, then?" Dale asked, dimly knowing already but wanting it in Topher's words anyway. That's what he'd been looking for, of course. Topher, to finally say it plain.

"It's mirth that keeps life and soul together, Dale. It's happiness. *That's* the philosopher's stone that keeps you young. Happiness, Dale."

Dale nodded vaguely, indicating he understood, even if he didn't entirely agree.

"Dominic Dromgoole said it –" Topher's words came bubbling up like a pure spring, burbling on musically like a stream – "I should have listened to him in the first place. He said the play is a paean to happiness. I didn't – I didn't have faith before, but now I –"

Topher stumbled to a verbal halt. He gazed searchingly at Dale – and when Dale found himself with nothing to say, Topher took hold of Dale's upper arms and shook him with gentle force.

"Your Life Plan," Topher said, somewhat more gently than he'd ever spoken of it before. "For fuck's sake, Dale," he continued in amused and reasonable tones. "Is there no room in there for happiness?"

Dale's throat felt alarmingly rusty. Panic spiked in him – he would be on again in a few minutes, with a long speech to deliver – and so he found himself answering, if only to reassure himself that he could. "Yes, I should … build that in. Happiness, I mean. I should schedule –"

Topher was grinning as if he'd won, and his hands slipped down to take Dale's hands and wrap them up warmly.

Dale wasn't ready for that yet, though. Dale wasn't ready for Topher winning. "I've got to – I'm on in a minute." His voice sounded rough, for any one of a number of reasons. "I need to gargle!"

And he dashed off for the dressing room, relieved at least that Topher had simply let him go with no protest.

◆

Interlude 4

After Merrythought had danced off and the musicians' tune came to a flourishing end, Nell sighed and stood up to stretch. Dale had often observed that the audience followed her in shifting on the hard wooden benches and rolling out the kinks in their shoulders. Watching a play in a Jacobean playhouse had physical aspects that weren't always pleasant or easy – though Dale had heard from more than a few people that the discomfort was simply considered to be part of the whole experience.

"Let them go, Georgie. That lazy old good-for-nothing shall not have any applause from us – nor a good word from anyone else in this company, if I have my way." She glared around at the audience, daring them to think well of Merrythought.

"No more he shall, love." Georgiana stood up beside her wife. "But, Nell, I will have Rafe do a very notable ceremony now, to the eternal honour and glory of all grocers."

Nell was aglow with excitement at the notion. "Oh, will you, Georgie?" she asked in breathless tones.

"I will, my love," Georgiana firmly replied. – "Sirrah! You there, boy! Can none of you back there hear me?"

Sam entered, his shoulders sagging dispiritedly. "Your pleasure, madam grocer?"

Georgiana was not at all daunted by his reluctant tones. "Sirrah, let Rafe come out on May Day in the morning, and speak while standing upon a fountain (which was put there by the City's worthies for the betterment of the people) – with all his scarfs about him, and his feathers, and his rings, and his baubles."

Sam somehow found the energy to be outraged. "Why, madam, do you never think of our plot? What will become of that? We are at a solemn place in the tale, you know, with life and death in the balance, and we cannot leave off to go a-maying."

"Why, sir, I do not care what becomes of your plot!" Georgiana angrily retorted. "I'll have Rafe come out, or I'll fetch him out myself, and I'll have something done in honour of the City. Besides, he has been long enough upon adventures. Bring him out quickly, or, if I come in amongst you –"

Sam had backed away from Georgiana's fury. "Well, madam, he shall come out, then – but if our play miscarries, madam, you are like to pay for it."

"Bring him on!"

Sam turned and left the stage with a quick step.

"This will be wonderful!" Nell happily declared. "Georgie, shall we have him do a morris dance, too, for the credit of the Strand?"

"No, sweetheart, it will be too much for the boy."

Rafe now entered through the main doors, in a hastily improvised May Lord's outfit, all in white, with green and red trimmings – some of the baubles a little too Christmassy, really, for a celebration of spring. He had a 'crown' of red poinsettias with their dark green leaves, borrowed from the restaurant's table decorations – which created a ripple of laughter from those audience members who had dined at the Swan before the show.

Tim and Frank each entered from the side doors, similarly attired as morris dancers, in white, with red and white ribbons for the flag of London and England, and bells chiming from round their calves.

"Oh, there he is, Nell!" said Georgiana. "Well, he looks reasonably good in his costume, but he is not wearing enough rings."

"He never was a one for bling," Nell remarked with wry fondness.

Rafe took centre stage, and delivered his speech, beginning in a respectful but relatively humble pose.

> "London, to thee I do present the merry month of
>   May;
> Let each true subject be content to hear me what I
>   say:
> For from the top of fountain-head, as plainly may
>   appear,
> I will both tell my name to you, and wherefore I
>   came here.

> "My name is Rafe, by due descent though not
>   ignoble me,
> Yet far inferior to the stock of gracious grocery;
> And by the common counsel of my fellows in the
>   Strand,
> With gilded staff and crossèd scarf, the May Lord
>   here I stand."

He stood tall and proud, and threw his arms wide to invite the whole audience, the whole of England, to join him in the revels.

> "Rejoice, oh, English hearts, rejoice! Rejoice, oh,
>   lovers dear!
> Rejoice, oh, city, town, and country! Rejoice, in
>   every shire!
> For now the fragrant flowers do spring and sprout in
>   seemly sort,
> The little birds do sit and sing, the lambs do make
>   fine sport.
>
> "And now the birchen-tree doth bud, that makes
>   the schoolboy weep;
> The morris rings, while hobby-horse doth foot it
>   daintily.
> The lords and ladies now abroad, for their disport
>   and play,
> Do kiss sometimes upon the grass, and sometimes
>   in the hay."

Tim and Frank had started dancing along in time with the rhythm, which made their bells jangle, but Rafe quelled them with a glance, and they resorted to waving their handkerchiefs over their heads instead. Much better. The next two lines involved Dale's favourite rhyme, after all.

> "Now little fish on tender stone begin to cast their
>   bellies,
> And sluggish snails, that erst were mute, do creep
>   out of their shellies.

The rumbling rivers now do warm, for little boys to
    paddle;
The sturdy steed now goes to grass, and up they
    hang his saddle.

"The heavy hart, the bellowing buck, the rascal, and
    the pricket,
Are now among the yeoman's peas, and leave the
    fearful thicket:
And be like them, oh, you, I say, of this same noble
    town,
Lifting up your velvet heads, and slipping off your
    gown."

"Wa-hay!" cried Tim in excitable agreement, tearing
open his shirt to reveal his scrawny chest. (There were a
few appreciative woots from the audience.)

"With bells on legs, and napkins clean unto your
    shoulders tied,
With scarfs and garters as you please, and 'Hey for
    our town!' cried.
March out, and show your willing minds, by twenty
    and by twenty,
To Hogsdon or to Newington, where ale and cakes
    are plenty.

"Up, then, I say, both young and old, both man and
    maid a-maying,
With sticks, and drums that bounce aloud, and
    merry tabor playing!

Which to prolong, God save our Queen, and send
    her country peace,
And root out treason from the land! And so, my
    friends, I cease."

Rafe took a bow to rapturous applause, and left the stage. Tim and Frank danced after him triumphantly, with bells a-jingling, and ribbons and handkerchiefs all a-flutter.

◆

Act Five

Venturewell entered, with a scroll of paper and a quill in his hands. "I will have no great store of company at the wedding," he mused as he consulted his handwritten lists; "a couple of neighbours and their wives. And we will have fine but modest fare: a capon in stewed broth, with marrow, and a good piece of beef stuck with rosemary."

Jasper crept onto the stage behind him, his face pale with flour and smoky dark smudges under his eyes. "Give up your plans, you foolish man! It is too late."

Venturewell leapt in fright. "Heaven bless me! Jasper!"

"Aye, I am his ghost, who you have injured for his constant love. You wretch! Who does not understand that true hearts cannot be parted by death?"

The old man quailed in fear of what he would now be told.

"Know you now that your daughter is quite borne away on wings of angels, through the liquid air, far beyond your reach, and never more shall you behold her face. She and I will in another world enjoy our loves; where neither father's anger, poverty, nor anything that troubles earthly men, shall sever our united hearts."

"Woe, woe, woe!" cried the bereft father.

"No, for she is made far happier than you ever cared to help her."

Venturewell moaned in grief.

Jasper thundered on: "Now never shall you sit or be alone in any place, but I will visit you with ghastly looks, and put into thy mind the great offences which you did me. When you are at your table with your friends, merry in heart, and filled with swelling wine, I'll come in the midst of all your pride and mirth, invisible to all men but yourself, and whisper a sad tale in your ear that shall make you let the cup fall from your hand, and stand as mute and pale as death itself."

"Forgive me, Jasper! Oh, what might I do, tell me, to satisfy your troubled ghost?"

"There are no means to satisfy me. It is too late to think of this."

"But tell me what it's best for me to do?"

"Repent your deed – and satisfy my poor father – and beat that fool Humphrey out of your house!"

As Venturewell collapsed to his knees and bowed low over his clasped hands, Jasper quickly and quietly left the stage through a side door.

"Did you hear that, Georgie?" Nell remarked in disgusted tones. "His very ghost would have folks beaten."

Humphrey now entered in some distress.

> "Father, my bride is gone, fair Mistress Luce:
> My soul's the fount of vengeance, mischief's sluice."

Venturewell wrenched himself up to his feet. "Hence, fool! Get out of my sight with your griefs and passions! You have undone me." And he battered at Humphrey's chest and shoulders with his fists.

"Hold off, my father dear, for Luce thy daughter's sake, who had no peer!"

"I am not your father, fool! There's some more blows. Begone!"

Humphrey stumbled out of reach, and stood there watching Venturewell warily with heaving breath.

Venturewell addressed the spirits of the air. "Jasper, I hope your ghost is well appeased to see your will performed. Now I will go to recompense your father for the wrongs I did you." And with that promise, a well humbled Venturewell left the stage.

Humphrey looked about him in bewilderment. "What shall I do? I have been beaten twice, and Mistress Luce is gone. Who is there left to help me?" He sighed, and his ridiculousness at last deflated. It was Humphrey's most honest moment. "My love is gone, and I never more will enjoy the light of the skies above, by day or by night. I will find a place in the dark, and wear out my soles and the stone beneath them, until the end relieves me of care."

As Humphrey left the stage, slumped and dejected, through the door on the right, the ever-cheerful Old Master Merrythought entered from the door on the left.

◆

When producing a 400-year-old play, Dale reflected, there were times when changes needed to be made. In between Humphrey exiting and Merrythought entering was a scene they had cut. The scene featured, at Nell's bidding, Rafe parading and drilling the local militia at Mile-End. There was much inept display – and even more innuendo and obscene references. Though if few in a modern-day audience would understand all the wordplay, then it became more obscure than obscene, and too much obscurity simply became pointless, which led to boredom. Not to mention the fact that many of the jokes were about the ghastly results of syphilis, which must have been a hell of a lot funnier in Beaumont's day. In this century, Dale felt it all went down like a lead balloon.

They had also cut an earlier scene that followed on from Rafe's defeat of Barbarossa, in which Rafe, Tim and Frank freed three knights and a woman held captive by the giant. The joke being that the four captives were actually syphilitic patients being tended by the barber-surgeon; their misadventures, symptoms and treatments were described in terms more appropriate to noble quests than ghastly reality. And again, Dale thought, the mix of sordid and chivalrous simply didn't seem so palatable these days.

In the spirit of audience participation, they had thought about recruiting four punters to play the Barber's four captives. Dale had loved the suggestion – from Topher, as it happened – that the audience members be rescued from 'Restricted View' seats, and perhaps placed on stools along the sides of the stage. After all, the original venue at Blackfriars would have had gentlemen seated on the stage, and the Citizens, too. In the end, the idea had been reluctantly let go, partly because the 'Restricted View' seats were by their nature a tad inaccessible, and partly because it was feared it would all be a bit too confronting for a mostly English audience.

Dale regretted that, however, and there was another thing he regretted even more. In cutting the scene in Act Five, one of his favourite lines had been lost – and that was:

"Gentleman, countrymen, friends, and my fellow-soldiers, I have brought you this day from the shops of security and the counters of content, to measure out in these furious fields honour by the ell, and prowess by the pound."

Delivering that would have been right grand, Dale thought, sighing wistfully.

◆

But, back to the play! The ever-cheerful Old Master Merrythought entered from the door on the left.

"Yet, I thank God, I bear not a wrinkle more than I had, and nor does age weigh me down. I have not a care in the world! My heart is as sound as an oak; and though I want drink to wet my whistle, I can still sing!

> *"Come no more there, boys, come no more there;*
> *For we shall never while we live come any more there."*

Now the messenger boy entered through the main doors, with the four men behind him carrying the coffin with its black-shrouded contents.

"God save you, sir!" cried the boy in greeting.

"Oh, you're a fair young fellow," Merrythought genially replied. "Can you sing?"

"Yes, sir, I can sing. But it is not so appropriate at this time."

> *"Sing we, and chant it;*
> *While love doth grant it."*

The boy shook his head in melancholy. "Sir – sir – if

you knew what I have brought here, you would have little wish to sing."

"Oh, the damsel round,
Full long I have thee sought,
And now I have thee found,
And what hast thou here brought?"

"A coffin, sir," replied the boy, "and your dead son Jasper in it."

With bowed heads, the boy and his attendants withdrew from the stage, with the doors closing fast behind them.

For a long moment Merrythought stood there still, as if finally stunned into silence. But at last he exclaimed, "Dead?" And then he sang in quietly heartfelt tones,

"Why, farewell he!
You were a bonny boy,
And I did love thee."

Meanwhile Jasper had entered through a side door, with his face clean and fresh again, and he said with warmth and affection, "Then, I pray you, sir, do so still."

"Jasper's ghost!" cried his father – before breaking into song one more.

"Thou art welcome from Stygian lake so soon.
Declare to me what wondrous things in Pluto's court are
  done."

Jasper laughed under his breath. "By my troth, sir, I never went there. It would be too hot for me."

Merrythought laughed happily. "A merry ghost, a very merry ghost!

"And where is your true love? Oh, where is your true love?"

"Look you here, sir!" Jasper lifted the cloth from the coffin, and then helped Luce out of it.

Once she was standing on the stage again, Merrythought grasped both her hands in his. "My bonny boy's darling girl!

"With hey, trixy, terlery-whiskin,
The world it runs on wheels.
When the young man's hands are a-friskin',
Up goes the maiden's heels."

There was a knocking at the main doors, and Mistress Merrythought called from within the tiring house, "What, Master Merrythought! Will you not let us in? What do you think shall become of us?"

Merrythought winked at Jasper, and sang out,

"What voice is that that calleth at our door?"

She replied in dry tones, "You know me well enough, sir; I am sure I have not been such a stranger to you these many years."

Master Merrythought once more sang his response.

"And some they whistled, and some they sung,
Hey, down, down!
And some did loudly say,
Ever as the Lord Barnet's horn blew,
Away, Musgrave, away!"

"You will not have your wife and child starve out here, will you, Master Merrythought?"

Jasper had listened to all this with a wry smile on his face. Now he pleaded sincerely, "Nay, good sir, be persuaded; she is my mother. Even if her offences have been great against you, let your own love remember she is yours, and so forgive her."

Luce chimed in, "Good Master Merrythought, let me entreat you; I will not be denied."

Mistress Merrythought called out again. "Why, Master Merrythought, will you remain vexed at me for all your life to come?"

"Woman," Merrythought cried in response, "I take you to my love again – but you shall sing before you enter this house. Therefore despatch your song and so come in."

"Well, you must have your will, when all's done," she loudly muttered. "Michael, what song can you sing?"

"I can sing none, forsooth, but 'A Lady's Daughter of Paris' properly."

"Aye, well that will do."

And Mistress Merrythought and Michael started up the song, with more courage than skill.

"It was a Lady's Daughter of Paris properly,
Her Mother her commanded to Mass that she should hie:
O pardon me, dear Mother, her Daughter dear did say,
Unto that filthy Idol I never can obey."

The main doors swung open, and in walked Mistress Merrythought and Michael. They were fondly greeted by Jasper and Luce, and Master Merrythought declared, "Come, you're welcome home again!

"If such danger be in playing,
And jest must to earnest turn,
You shall go no more a-maying –"

His song was interrupted by more loud knocking at the main doors, and Venturewell called out from within the tiring house. "Are you at home, sir? Master Merrythought!"

Jasper said quietly to his father, "It is my master's voice. Good sir, go hold him in talk, while we hide ourselves in another room." He and Luce quickly exited through a side door.

"What are you?" called Merrythought. "Are you merry, sir? You must be very merry, if you want to enter."

"I am, sir."

"Sing me a song, then."

Venturewell was understandably reluctant. "Nay, good sir, open to me."

"Sing, I say, or, by the merry heart, you come not in!"

"Well then, sir, I'll sing.

The doors swung open once more, and in came Venturewell.

"You are welcome, sir," said Merrythought, "you are welcome. You see your entertainment; pray you, be merry."

But Venturewell was too distraught to be merry. He doffed his hat and wrung it in both hands. "Oh, Master Merrythought, I'm come to ask you forgiveness for the wrongs I offered you and your most virtuous son! My wrongs are infinite; yet my contrition shall be more than my wrongs. I do confess that my hardness broke his heart, for which Heaven has justly given me punishment – more punishment than my age can carry. His wandering spirit, not yet at rest, pursues me everywhere, crying, 'I'll haunt thee for thy cruelty.' My daughter, she is gone, I know not how, taken invisible, and whether living or in the grave, it is yet uncertain to me. Oh, Master Merrythought, these are the weights that will sink me to my grave! Forgive me, sir."

Merrythought, now knowing all, beamed at him. "Why, sir, I *do* forgive you. Be merry! And if my son in his lifetime played the knave, can you forgive him, too?"

"With all my heart, sir," Venturewell averred.

Merrythought was almost bubbling over with mirth. "Speak it again, and heartily."

"I do, sir! Now, by my soul, I do."

Merrythought again burst into song:

"With that came out his paramour;
She was as white as the lily flower.
Hey, troll, trollie, lollie!"

Luce and Jasper returned to the stage, and were reconciled with a desperately relieved Venturewell, while Merrythought continued his song.

"With that came out her own dear knight;
He was as true as e'er did fight.
Hey, troll, trollie, lollie!

"Sir," said Merrythought, "if you will forgive them, join their hands together, and there's no more to be said in the matter."

The young couple glowed with quietly confident happiness, the sort that might well last them all their lives together.

"I do, I do gladly forgive them," said Venturewell, taking Luce's and Jasper's hands in his and putting them together, blessing their betrothal by this act. The warmth of beneficence and love swelled every heart in the house –

– "I do *not* like this!" cried Georgiana, standing at the foot of the stage and cutting across *The London Merchant*'s happy ending. "Peace!"

The action ground to a halt, and everyone stared at her with smiles fixed or falling.

"Listen. Everybody's part has come to an end except Rafe's, and he's left out."

Sam ventured onto the stage. "That's not our fault, madam grocer. We have nothing to do with his part."

"Rafe, come out here!" Georgiana called. She said to the assembled actors, "Help him to an ending, my fine fellows, as you have done with the rest. Come on."

Nell, of course, had a grand idea. "Now, my wife, let Rafe come out and die."

"He shall, Nell. – Rafe, come out here now, and die!"

The other actors sagged at the notion, and Sam complained, "It won't do, madam, when there is no good *reason* for him to die, and it is hardly befitting at the end of a comedy."

"Never mind all that," said Georgiana. "Will his part not be at an end when he's dead?"

Sam looked at the other players, and they all nodded wearily, as if somewhat gladdened by the thought that this evening might indeed come to an end at some point.

"Come on, Rafe!"

And then Dale had the privilege of performing the funniest visual gag ever in the history of theatre. It had taken him a week of rehearsals to be able to do it with a suitably earnest face.

Rafe entered through the main doors in his regular clothes – with a forked arrow through his head – and strode to the centre of the stage before taking up his best speechifying pose.

The audience collapsed in hysterical laughter.

Rafe stood there, absolutely straight-faced, waiting them out.

After a long moment, Dale tweaked his pose into something even nobler, and created a fresh wave of hysterics. Something within him, the place deep down in his gut where his true emotions remained safely hidden, was laughing, too – and it was tempting to share that, especially on this, the last night of the run.

But he decided that wouldn't be fair. It was the best damned gag ever – Rafe walking out to deliver a soliloquy *with a fucking forked arrow through his head* – and Dale wanted everyone to enjoy the moment for all it was worth.

The actors who were on stage were a mix of wry humour and exhaustion, while the other actors who hadn't been on stage either stepped out to be part of the fun or poked their heads around the doors or over the balustrade to see what was going on.

Finally Dale judged that enough was enough – and Rafe lifted a surprisingly graceful hand, and began his speech.

> "When I was mortal, this my costive corpse
> Did lap up figs and raisins in the Strand;
> Where sitting, I espied a lovely dame,
> Whose master wrought with lingel and with awl,
> And underground he resoled many a boot.
>
> "Straight did her love prick forth me, tender sprig,
> To follow feats of arms in warlike wise
> Through Waltham-desert – where I did perform
> Many achievements, and did lay on ground
> Huge Barbarossa, that bragging giant.
>
> "Then honour pricked me from my native soil
> Into Moldavia, where I gained the love
> Of Pompiona, the king's belovèd daughter;
> But yet proved constant to the black-thumbed maid

Susan, and scornèd Pompiona's love.
Yet liberal I was, and gave her pins,
And money for her father's officers."

Rafe took a step forward, and lay his hand over his heart with simple sincerity. Every soul in the audience was focussed entirely on him, with their breath stopped in their mouths.

"I then returnèd home, and thrust myself
In action, and by all men chosen was
Lord of the May, where I did flourish it,
With scarfs and rings, and posy on my head.
But all these things I, Rafe, did undertake
Only for my belovèd Susan's sake.

"Then coming home, and sitting in my shop
With apron blue – Death came into my stall
To bargain for *aqua vitae*. But ere I
Could take the bottle down and fill a taste,
Death caught a pound of pepper in his hand,
And sprinkled all my face and body o'er
And in an instant vanishèd away."

Georgiana nodded approvingly, and murmured, "It is a pretty story, in faith." Rafe wobbled a little, and his hand clutched at his chainmail tunic, but he determinedly continued on.

"Then took I up my bow and shaft in hand,
And walkèd into Moorfields to cool myself.

But there grim cruel Death met me again,
And shot this forkèd arrow through my head;
And now I faint …"

Rafe slowly collapsed down to the stage, supported in the arms of Mistress Merrythought and Michael. All the other actors on the stage were moved by now, and focussed solely on this pitiable death scene. Tim and Frank rushed forward to take one of Rafe's hands in theirs.

"Farewell, all you good boys in merry London!
Ne'er shall we more upon Shrove-Tuesday meet,
And pluck down houses of iniquity. –
My pain increases! – I shall never more
Play 'Ride the wild mare' nor dance,
Nor daub a satin gown with rotten eggs –
Oh, never more shall I! I die!
Fly, fly, my soul, to Grocers' Hall!"

And with several gut-deep moans (the dialogue literally read 'O, O, O, &c.') Rafe expired, to the grief of all.

A quiet, still moment passed.

Then Nell burst into loud applause. "Well said, Rafe! Well said!" The audience followed her lead, adding a few whoops for good measure. Rafe got to his feet, and stood there looking a little stunned.

Once she could be heard again, Nell continued, "Do your obeisance to the ladies and gentlemen, and go your ways. Well said, Rafe!"

Amid ongoing applause, Rafe took the arrow from off his head, and handed it to Frank – and then took his bows, before making his way back down to the Pit to sit beside Nell and Georgiana. He appeared a little sad that it was over, but also pleased, and far more grounded and confident than he had been at the start of the evening.

As the audience resettled and began looking about wondering what (if anything) might happen next, Master Merrythought stepped forward. "Methinks all we, thus kindly and unexpectedly reconciled, should not depart without a song."

"A good motion," cried Venturewell.

"Strike up, then!"

The musicians launched into a by now familiar tune, and the company took their places on stage to join in the song – with Rafe and the Citizens gazing up at them, and clapping along to the music with delight.

> *"Better music ne'er was known*
> *Than a quire of hearts in one.*
> *Let each other, that hath been*
> *Troubled with the gall or spleen,*
> *Learn of us to keep his brow*
> *Smooth and plain, as ours are now:*
> *Sing, though before the hour of dying;*
> *He shall rise, and then be crying,*
> *'Hey, ho, 'tis nought but mirth*
> *That keeps the body from the earth!'"*

The company took their bows to thunderous applause, and exited through into the tiring house.

◆

Epilogue

Georgiana immediately stood to keep the audience in their seats for one speech more. "Come, Nell, shall we go? The play is done."

Nell stood to join her, while Rafe remained seated. "Nay, by my faith, Georgie, I have more manners than that. I'll speak to these lovely people first." She took her by-now-accustomed spot at the foot of the stage, and turned around with arms spread, to address the audience on all sides. "I thank you, ladies and gentlemen, for your patience and for your encouragement of Rafe, a poor fatherless child. And if I might see you at my house, I would have a bottle of wine and a pipe of tobacco for you. For, truly, I hope you do like the youth, but I would be glad to know the truth. I refer it to your own discretions, whether you will applaud him or not; for I will wink, and meanwhile you shall do what you will."

With Nell's encouragement, Rafe stood up and took his bows again, to happy applause.

"I thank you with all my heart," cried Nell. "God give you good night! – Come, Georgie."

And the three of them made their way down through the Pit.

Exeunt.

♦

The Jig

Of course no play at the Globe or the Playhouse could be allowed to end without a jig.

The company poured back out onto the stage to further applause, the musicians struck up a rowdy 'Chicken Dance', and with much joyous laughter shared with the audience, the actors all began to dance along. Their body language now transformed to their own, but their interactions with the other cast members played with their characters' relationships as well as their own.

Merrythought and Venturewell danced together as reconciled friends, before Merrythought switched to Mistress Merrythought and Michael. Tim and Frank energetically performed their own version of the dance, caught up together in their own little world. The Citizens and Rafe – or, rather, Dale – came running back up through the Pit, and joined the rest of the company on stage.

As the musical bridge began, they all partnered up to dance a polka, merrily getting in each other's way on the small stage.

Dale was supposed to dance with Sam, while the play's acknowledged couples – Georgiana and Nell, the Merrythoughts, and Jasper and Luce (though the latter were now recognisable instead as Topher and Verity) – all spun off together. Tim danced around with Frank sitting perched on his shoulders. Venturewell danced with his friend Humphrey (now obviously Jeremy, a Celebrity), while Michael danced with the Tapster.

Well, that wouldn't do tonight.

Dale bowed an apology to Sam, and strode over to tap Verity on the shoulder. She was startled, of course. Sure, they'd all been in a play which involved audience members trying to take over as directors and creating an impromptu play of their own, but that didn't mean the cast were ready to go off-script for real. But – "May I cut in?" Dale asked.

Verity glanced at Topher, and saw that this wasn't unwelcome, so she gave up her partner with a good grace. Dale slid into her place, and let Topher lead them back into the dance. Who knew which one of them was grinning more madly?

And of course Jeremy wasn't going to let his lady love be abandoned, so before Sam could step in, Jeremy ditched Venturewell and went to offer his services. Verity seemed happy enough at the switch, and when Dale next saw her she looked thoughtful as if she'd finally spied the truth of Jeremy's feelings.

Sam and Venturewell partnered up with a philosophical shrug, and so they all carried on, round and round in a whirl.

As the company took their final bows, the order in which the main actors stood was forced to change a little, as Dale refused to let go of Topher's hand. The audience were cheering and hooting, and the applause was so hard that it thrummed through the wooden floor. Dale felt indescribably giddy with happiness, as if in these moments anything were possible.

There was one last bit of business to perform, however. The actors turned as one and lifted their arms to direct the applause towards the musicians – who stood and took their bows. And then the company all took a step to either side to reveal the centre of the stage, and lowered their arms to direct the audience's attention to the Hellmouth, the trapdoor in the centre of the stage, which was now open.

After a moment, a tall hat with a feathery garnish popped up, and then a man peered out shyly. The actors beckoned encouragingly, and applauded, and finally he scrambled up onto the stage. He was dressed in proper, sober Jacobean garb, and carried a rolled-up scroll and a quill in his hands – but just in case he wasn't recognised, Dale announced, "Ladies and gentlemen, the poet and playwright, Mr Francis Beaumont!"

The audience and company joined together in an enthusiastic storm of cheers and whistles, clapping and stomping.

Beaumont seemed surprised and (quite naturally) delighted by this enthusiastic reception. He bowed low in humble gratitude. He was only a young man, Dale reflected. Beaumont had died untimely at the age of thirty-two – and *The Knight of the Burning Pestle* had been produced for only one performance in his lifetime, and had been considered a failure. Well, no more of that!

As Beaumont smiled warmly – nay, beatifically – he gently ascended through the air towards the Heavens, wafted up by the laughter and appreciation, until eventually he disappeared through the trapdoor into a happier afterlife.

The company took one last bow, and then at last the evening was over, the actors made their way backstage – and the audience were treated to a glimpse, as the main doors slowly swung closed, of Topher kissing Dale, of Jasper kissing Rafe. And all were reconciled and joined, each to the other, from the very depths of their hearts.

◆

Backstage and Beyond

The giddy jig continued backstage as everyone raised a drink to Dale and Topher, and declared that they knew all along how it must be – "He's the irresistible force to your immovable object!" Nell told Dale.

"Which makes him perfect for you," added Georgiana.

"The earth turns, and you begin your new journey," said Merrythought. "There can be no more auspicious time of year."

The company cried merry farewells to all their friends as they divested themselves of their costumes, before gathering up the last of their belongings and dashing out into the night to catch the Tube home.

Dale wasn't ready to go home yet – or, perhaps more to the point, to work out whether they should go to Topher's home instead. The moment was still full of magical possibilities, and Dale wanted to remain within it for as long as he could.

So, instead, he and Topher stole out through a side exit of the Globe, and walked hand-in-hand along the Thames towards the Tate, and then up onto Millennium Bridge. Topher must have shared Dale's sense of wonder, for they both naturally came to a halt about halfway along, and stood there leaning against the railings, looking downriver.

The night was dark, but London's lights were eternally bright. Reflections were cast on the water by Southwark Bridge, the railway bridge, London Bridge, Tower Bridge – and then the patches of light danced about in the wake of a passing ferry. The white walls of the Globe were still lit up on their right, and further down the river, the glassy Shard pierced the sky. To the left was the dome of St Paul's, symbolic of all that was London.

"I love this place," Topher fervently murmured – and then he tensed a little, as if suddenly aware that he'd just said the L word, and maybe it was way too soon for that.

Dale chuckled under his breath and grasped Topher's hand tighter. "Aye," he agreed. And then, because words had now been spoken, no matter how irrelevant, Dale continued, "You know … I might have been taking myself a tad too seriously, with my Grand Life Plan and all that."

Topher tried to muffle a laugh, and totally failed. "You think?" he asked lightly.

"I think I'll always be ambitious. But … you're right, there's more to life, there are other things as well. Sometimes, maybe, doing things with no purpose, or even not doing anything … is a proper purpose after all." He frowned, reaching for something he'd learned or maybe re-learned that night. "It's, like, the Citizens as … as unreliable narrators. You know? That's not quite it – but it's not that the author of *The London Merchant* had taken the Citizens into account either, yeah? Everything we see is skewed by our own worldview."

Topher was watching him, hardly even daring to breathe, as if sensing how fundamental all this was, no matter how confused Dale sounded.

"I'm really not sure what I'm getting at here," Dale confessed with a grin, turning to face this man, his friend, his … lover. "But maybe that it's time I considered other priorities, yeah? I mean, as well. Yours as well as mine."

"Yeah," Topher whispered at last. "That works, Dale, that's good. Actually, that's fucking magnificent!"

Dale's breath shimmered in the air as if the laughter truly had been infectious, and then he drew close to Topher and quietly sang,

> *"Hey, ho, 'tis nought but mirth*
> *That keeps the body from the earth!"*

And they kissed, clasping each other close, together there in the heart of their home city, and their shared lives were remade anew.

Finis.

About Julie Bozza

I was born in England and lived most of my life in Australia before returning to the UK some years ago; my dual nationality means that I am often a bit too cheeky, but will always apologize for it.

I have been writing fiction for over thirty years, mostly for the enjoyment of myself and my friends, but writing is my love and my vocation so of course that's where my dreams and ambitions are. In the meantime, technical writing helps to pay the mortgage, while I also have fun with web design, reading, watching movies and television, knitting, and imbibing espresso.

Other titles by Julie Bozza:
The Apothecary's Garden
Butterfly Hunter
Of Dreams and Ceremonies
The Thousand Smiles of Nicholas Goring
A Certain Persuasion (anthology)
The Definitive Albert J. Sterne
Albert J. Sterne: Future Bright, Past Imperfect
The Fine Point of His Soul
Homosapien … a fantasy about pro wrestling
Mitch Rebecki Gets a Life
A Pride of Poppies (anthology)
A Threefold Cord
The 'True Love' Solution
The Valley of the Shadow of Death

For more, please visit juliebozza.com and libra-tiger.com

A Night with the Knight of the Burning Pestle

by Francis Beaumont and Julie Bozza

Dale is proud of how his acting career is progressing. Tonight, for instance, is the last night (at the beautiful Sam Wanamaker Playhouse) of a well-received run of Beaumont's *The Knight of the Burning Pestle*, in which he plays Rafe. But his colleague Topher, who plays Jasper, seems to think something is missing in Dale's life. They're not really friends, and Dale sees little point in reprising the one night on which they were not-really-friends with benefits.

However! Despite the distractions of performing this chaotic two-plays-within-a-play, Dale is plagued by the niggling doubts prompted by Topher. Dale might be better off paying attention, though – because maybe Francis Beaumont, writing over 400 years ago, already provided the answers to Dale's dilemma.